经典的回声·ECHO OF

林家铺子
THE SHOP OF THE LIN FAMILY

春 蚕
SPRING SILKWORMS

茅 盾 著
沙博理 译

Written by Mao Dun
Translated by Sidney Shapiro

外文出版社
FOREIGN LANGUAGES PRESS

图书在版编目(CIP)数据

林家铺子 春蚕:汉英对照/茅盾著;—北京:外文出版社,2001
(经典的回声)
ISBN 7-119-02777-8

Ⅰ.①林...②春... Ⅱ.茅... Ⅲ.英语-对照读物,小说-汉、英 Ⅳ.H319.4:I

中国版本图书馆 CIP 数据核字(2000)第 78571 号

外文出版社网址:
http://www.flp.com.cn
外文出版社电子信箱:
info@flp.com.cn
sales@flp.com.cn

经典的回声
林家铺子 春蚕(汉英对照)

作　　者	茅　盾
译　　者	沙博理
责任编辑	刘春英　刘新航
封面设计	陈　军
出版发行	外文出版社
社　　址	北京市百万庄大街24号　邮政编码　100037
电　　话	(010)68320579(总编室)
	(010)68329514/68327211(推广发行部)
印　　刷	北京市通县大中印刷厂
经　　销	新华书店/外文书店
开　　本	大32开(850×1168毫米)　字　数　94千字
印　　数	0001—8000册　印　张　7
版　　次	2001年1月第1版第1次印刷
装　　别	平　装
书　　号	ISBN 7-119-02777-8/I.446(外)
定　　价	13.00元

版权所有　侵权必究

出 版 前 言

　　本社专事外文图书的编辑出版,几十年来用英文翻译出版了大量的中国文学作品和文化典籍,上自先秦,下迄现当代,力求全面而准确地反映中国文学及中国文化的基本面貌和灿烂成就。这些英译图书均取自相关领域著名的、权威的作品,英译则出自国内外译界名家。每本图书的编选、翻译过程均极其审慎严肃,精雕细琢,中文作品及相应的英译版本均堪称经典。

　　我们意识到,这些英译精品,不单有对外译介的意义,而且对国内英文学习者、爱好者及英译工作者,也是极有价值的读本。为此,我们对这些英译精品做了认真的遴选,编排成汉英对照的形式,陆续推出,以飨读者。

外文出版社

Publisher's Note

Foreign Languages Press is dedicated to the editing, translating and publishing of books in foreign languages. Over the past several decades it has published, in English, a great number of China's classics and records as well as literary works from the Qin down to modern times, in the aim to fully display the best part of the Chinese culture and its achievements. These books in the original are famous and authoritative in their respective fields, and their English translations are masterworks produced by notable translators both at home and abroad. Each book is carefully compiled and translated with minute precision. Consequently, the English versions as well as their Chinese originals may both be rated as classics.

It is generally considered that these English translations are not only significant for introducing China to the outside world but also useful reading materials for domestic English learners and translators. For this reason, we have carefully selected some of these books, and will publish them successively in Chinese-English bilingual form.

Foreign Languages Press

目 录
CONTENTS

林家铺子　　　　　　　　　　　　1
春　　蚕　　　　　　　　　　　137

THE SHOP OF THE LIN FAMILY   3

SPRING SILKWORMS   139

茅盾像
The picture of Mao Dun

林家铺子

THE SHOP OF THE LIN FAMILY

一

林小姐这天从学校回来就撅起着小嘴唇。她掼下了书包,并不照例到镜台前梳头发搽粉,却倒在床上看着帐顶出神。小花噗的也跳上床来,挨着林小姐的腰部摩擦,咪呜咪呜地叫了两声。林小姐本能地伸手到小花头上摸了一下,随即翻一个身,把脸埋在枕头里,就叫道:

"妈呀!"

没有回答。妈的房就在间壁,妈素常疼爱这唯一的女儿,听得女儿回来就要摇摇摆摆走过来问她肚子饿不饿,妈留着好东西呢,——再不然,就差吴妈赶快去买一碗馄饨。但今天却作怪,妈的房里明明有说话的声音,并且还听得妈在打呃,却是妈连回答也没有一声。

林小姐在床上又翻一个身,翘起了头,打算偷听妈和谁谈话,是那样悄地放低了声音。

I

Miss Lin's small mouth was pouting when she returned home from school that day. She flung down her books, and instead of combing her hair and powdering her nose before the mirror as usual, she stretched out on the bed. Her eyes staring at the top of the bed canopy, Miss Lin lay lost in thought. Her little cat leaped up beside her, snuggled against her waist and miaowed twice. Automatically, she patted his head, then rolled over and buried her face in the pillow.

"Ma!" called Miss Lin.

No answer. Ma, whose room was right next door, ordinarily doted on this only daughter of hers. On hearing her return, Ma would come swaying in to ask whether she was hungry. Ma would be keeping something good for her. Or she might send the maid out to buy a bowl of hot soup with meat dumplings from a street vendor. . . . But today was odd. There obviously were people talking in Ma's room—Miss Lin could hear Ma hiccuping too—yet Ma didn't even reply.

Again Miss Lin rolled over on the bed, and raised her head She would eavesdrop on this conversation. Whom could Ma be talking to, that voices had to be kept so low?

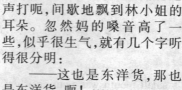

然而听不清,只有妈的连声打呃,间歇地飘到林小姐的耳朵。忽然妈的嗓音高了一些,似乎很生气,就有几个字听得很分明:

——这也是东洋货,那也是东洋货,呃!……

林小姐猛一跳,就好像理发时候颈脖子上粘了许多短头发似的浑身都烦躁起来了。正也是为了这东洋货问题,她在学校里给人家笑骂,她回家来没好气。她一手推开了又挨到她身边来的小花,跳起来就剥下那件新制的翠绿色假毛葛驼绒旗袍来,拎在手里抖了几下,叹一口气。据说这怪好看的假毛葛和驼绒都是东洋来的。她撩开这件驼绒旗袍,从床下拖出那口小巧的牛皮箱来,赌气似的扭开了箱子盖,把箱子底朝天向床上一撒,花花绿绿的衣服和杂用品就滚满了一床。小花吃了一惊,噗的跳下床去,转一个身,却又跳在一张椅子上蹲着望住它的女主人。

林小姐的一双手在那堆衣服里抓捞了一会儿,就呆呆地站在床前出神。这许多衣服和杂用品越看越可爱,却又越看越像是东洋货呢!全都不能穿

But she couldn't make out what they were saying. Only Ma's continuous hiccups wafted intermittently to Miss Lin's ears, Suddenly, Ma's voice rose, as if she were angry, and a few words came through quite clearly:

"—These are Japanese goods, those are Japanese goods, hic!..."

Miss Lin started. She prickled all over, like when she was having a hair-cut and the tiny shorn hairs stuck to her neck. She had come home annoyed just because they had laughed at her and scolded her at school over Japanese goods. She swept aside the little cat nestled against her, jumped up and stripped off her new azure rayon dress lined with camel's wool. She shook it out a couple of times, and sighed. Miss Lin had heard that this charming frock was made of Japanese material. She tossed it aside and pulled that cute cowhide case out from under the bed. Almost spitefully, she flipped the cover open, and turning the case upside down, dumped its contents on the bed. A rainbow of brightly coloured dresses and knick-knacks rolled and spread. The little cat leaped to the floor, whirled and jumped up on a chair, where he crouched and looked at his mistress in astonishment.

Miss Lin sorted through the pile of clothes, then stood, abstracted, beside the bed. The more she examined her belongings, the more she adored them— and the more they looked like Japanese goods! Couldn't

了么?可是她——舍不得,而且她的父亲也未必肯另外再制新的!林小姐忍不住眼圈儿红了。她爱这些东洋货,她又恨那些东洋人;好好儿的发兵打东三省干么呢?不然,穿了东洋货有谁来笑骂。

"呃——"

忽然房门边来了这一声。接着就是林大娘的摇摇摆摆的瘦身形。看见那乱丢了一床的衣服,又看见女儿只穿着一件绒线短衣站在床前出神,林大娘这一惊非同小可。心里愈是着急,她那个"呃"却愈是打得多,暂时竟说不出半句话。

林小姐飞跑到母亲身边,哭丧着脸说:

"妈呀!全是东洋货,明儿叫我穿什么衣服?"

林大娘摇着头只是打呃,一手扶住了女儿的肩膀,一手揉磨自己的胸脯,过了一会儿,她方才挣扎出几句话来:

"阿囡,呃,你干么脱得——呃,光落落?留心冻——呃——我这毛病,呃,生你那年起了这个病痛,呃,近来越发凶了!呃——"

"妈呀!你说明儿我穿什么衣服?我只好躲在家里不出去了,他们要笑我,骂我!"

she wear any of them? She hated to part with them—besides, her father wouldn't necessarily be willing to have new ones made for her! Miss Lin's eyes began to smart. She loved these Japanese things, while she hated the Japanese aggressors who invaded the Northeast provinces. If not for that, she could wear Japanese merchandise and no one would say a word.

"Hic—"

The sound came through the door, followed by the thin swaying body of Mrs. Lin. The sight of the heap of clothing on the bed, and her daughter, bemused, standing in only her brief woollen underwear, was more than a little shock. As her excitement increased, the tempo of Mrs. Lin's hiccups grew in proportion. For the moment, she was unable to speak. Miss Lin, grief written all over her face, flew to her mother. "Ma! They're all Japanese goods. What am I going to wear tomorrow?"

Hiccuping, Mrs. Lin shook her head. With one hand she supported herself on her daughter's shoulder, with the other she kneaded her own chest. After a while, she managed to force out a few sentences.

"Child—hic—why have you taken off—hic—all your clothes? The weather's cold—hic—This trouble of mine—hic—began the year you were born. Hic—lately it's getting worse! Hic—"

"Ma, tell me what am I going to wear tomorrow?

但是林大娘不回答。她一路打呃，走到床前拣出那件驼绒旗袍来，就替女儿披在身上，又拍拍床，要她坐下。小花又挨到林小姐脚边，昂起了头，眯细着眼睛看看林大娘，又看看林小姐；然后它懒懒地靠到林小姐的脚背上，就林小姐的鞋底来磨擦它的肚皮。林小姐一脚踢开了小花，就势身子一歪，躺在床上，把脸藏在她母亲的身后。

暂时两个都没有话。母亲忙着打呃，女儿忙着盘算"明天怎样出去"；这东洋货问题不但影响到林小姐的所穿，还影响到她的所用；据说她那只常为同学们艳羡的化妆皮夹以及自动铅笔之类，也都是东洋货，而她却又爱这些小玩意儿的！

"阿囡，呃——肚子饿不饿？"林大娘坐定了半晌以后，渐渐少打几个呃了，就又开始她日常的疼爱女儿的老功课。

"不饿。嗳，妈呀，怎么老是问我饿不饿呢，顶要紧是没有了衣服明天怎样去上学！"

林小姐撒娇说，依然那样拳曲着身体躺着，依然把脸藏

I'll just hide in the house and not go out! They'll laugh at me, swear at me!"

Mrs. Lin didn't answer. Hiccuping steadily, she walked over to the bed, picked the new azure dress out of the pile, and draped it over her daughter. Then she patted the bed in invitation for Miss Lin to sit down. The little cat returned to beside the girl's legs. Cocking his head, with narrowed eyes he looked first at Mrs. Lin, then at her daughter. Lazily, he rolled over and rubbed his belly against the soles of the girl's shoes. Miss Lin kicked him away and reclined sideways on the bed, with her head hidden behind her mother's back.

Neither of them spoke for a while. Mrs. Lin was busy hiccuping; her daughter was busy calculating "how to go out tomorrow." The problem of Japanese goods not only affected everything Miss Lin wore—it influenced everything she used. Even the powder compact which her fellow students so admired and her automatic pencil were probably made in Japan. And she was crazy about those little gadgets!

"Child—hic—are you hungry?"

After sitting quietly for some time, Mrs. Lin gradually controlled her hiccups, and began her usual doting routine.

"No. Ma, why do you always ask me if I'm hungry? The most important thing is that I have no clothes. How can I go to school tomorrow?" the girl demanded petulantly. She was still curled up on the bed, her face

在母亲背后。

自始就没弄明白为什么女儿尽嚷着没有衣服穿的林大娘现在第三次听得了这话儿,不能不再注意了,可是她那该死的打呃很不作美地又连连来了。恰在此时林先生走了进来,手里拿着一张字条儿,脸上乌霉霉地像是涂着一层灰。他看见林大娘不住地打呃,女儿躺在满床乱丢的衣服堆里,他就料到了几分,一双眉头就紧紧地皱起。他唤着女儿的名字说道:

"明秀,你的学校里有什么抗日会么?刚送来了这封信。说是明天你再穿东洋货的衣服去,他们就要烧呢——无法无天的话语,咳……"

"呃——呃!"

"真是岂有此理,哪一个人身上没有东洋货,却偏偏找定了我们家来生事!哪一家洋广货铺子里不是堆足了东洋货,偏是我的铺子犯法,一定要封存!咄!"

林先生气愤愤地又加了这几句,就颓然坐在床边的一张椅子里。

"呢,呃,救苦救难观世音,呃——"

"爸爸,我还有一件老式的棉袄,光景不是东洋货,可是穿出去人家又要笑我。"

10

still buried behind her mother.

From the start, Mrs. Lin hadn't understood why her daughter kept complaining that she had no clothes to wear. This was the third time and she couldn't ignore the remark any longer, but those damned hiccups most irritatingly started up again. Just then, Mr. Lin came in. He was holding a sheet of paper in his hand; his face was ashen. He saw his wife struggling with continuous agitated hiccups, his daughter lying on the clothing-strewn bed, and he could guess pretty well what was wrong. His brows drew together in a frown.

"Do you have an Anti-Japanese-Invasion Society in your school, Xiu?" he asked. "This letter just came. It says that if you wear clothes made of Japanese material again tomorrow, they're going to burn them! Of all the wild lawless things to say!"

"Hic—hic!"

"What nonsense! Everyone has something made in Japan on him. But they have to pick on our family to make trouble! There isn't a shop carrying foreign goods that isn't full of Japanese stuff. But they have to make our shop the culprit. They insist on locking up our stocks! Huh!"

"Hic—hic—Goddess Kuanyin protect and preserve us! Hic—"

"Papa, I've got an old style padded jacket. It's probably not made of Japanese material, but if I wear it they'll all laugh at me, it's so out of date," said Miss

过了一会儿,林小姐从床上坐起来说,她本来打算进一步要求父亲制一件不是东洋货的新衣,但瞧着父亲的脸色不对,便又不敢冒昧。同时,她的想象中就展开了那件旧棉袄惹人讪笑的情形,她忍不住哭起来了。

"呃,呃——啊哟!——呃,莫哭,——没有人笑你——呃,阿囡……"

"阿秀,明天不用去读书了!饭快要没得吃了,还读什么书!"

林先生懊恼地说,把手里那张字条儿扯得粉碎,一边走出房去,一边叹气跺脚。然而没多几时,林先生又匆匆地跑了回来,看着林大娘的面孔说道:

"橱门上的钥匙呢?给我!"

林大娘的脸色立刻变成灰白,瞪出了眼睛望着她的丈夫,永远不放松她的打呃忽然静定了半晌。

"没有办法,只好去斋斋那些闲神野鬼了——"

林先生顿住了,叹一口气,然后又接下去说:

"至多我花四百块。要是党部里还嫌少,我拼着不做生意,等他们来封!——我们对过的裕昌祥,进的东洋货比我多,足足有一万多块钱的码子呢,也只花了五百块,就太平无事了。——五百块!算是吃了

12

Lin, sitting up on the bed. She had been thinking of going a step farther and asking Mr. Lin to have a dress made for her out of non-Japanese cloth, but his expression decided her against such a rash move. Still, picturing the jeers her old padded jacket would evoke, she couldn't restrain her tears.

"Hic—hic—child! —hic—don't cry—no one will laugh at you—hic—child...."

"Xiu, you don't have to go to school tomorrow! We soon won't have anything to eat; how can we spend money on schools!" Mr. Lin was exasperated. He ripped up the letter and strode, sighing, from the room. Before long, he came hurrying back.

"Where's the key to the cabinet? Give it to me!" he demanded of his wife.

Mrs. Lin turned pale and stared at him. Her eternal hiccups were momentarily stilled.

"There's no help for it. We'll have to make an offering to those straying demons—" Mr. Lin paused to heave a sigh. "It'll cost me four hundred at most. If the Kuomintang local branch thinks it's not enough, I'll quit doing business. Let them lock up the stocks! That shop opposite has more Japanese goods than I. They've made an investment of over ten thousand dollars. They paid out only five hundred, and they're going along without a bit of trouble. Five hundred dollars! Just mark it off as a couple of bad debts! —The key! That

几笔倒账罢!——钥匙!咳!那一个金项圈,总可以兑成三百块……"

"呃,呃,真——好比强盗!"

林大娘摸出那钥匙来,手也颤抖了,眼泪扑簌簌地往下掉。林小姐却反不哭了,瞪着一对泪眼,呆呆地出神,她恍惚看见那个曾经到她学校里来演说而且饿狗似的盯住看她的什么委员,一个怪叫人讨厌的黑麻子,捧住了她家的金项圈在半空里跳,张开了大嘴巴笑。随后,她又恍惚看见这强盗似的黑麻子和她的父亲吵嘴,父亲被他打了,……

"啊哟!"

林小姐猛然一声惊叫,就扑在她妈的身上。林大娘慌得没有工夫尽打呃,挣扎着说:

"阿囡,呃,不要哭,——过了年,你爸爸有钱,就给你制新衣服,——呃,那些狠心的强盗!都咬定我们有钱,呃,一年一年亏空,你爸爸做做肥田粉生意又上当,呃——店里全是别人的钱了。阿囡,呃,呃,我这病,活着也受罪,——呃,再过两年,你十九岁,招得个好女婿。呃,我死也放心了!——救苦救难观世音菩萨!呃——"

gold necklace ought to bring about three hundred....

"Hic—hic—really, like a gang of robbers!" Mrs. Lin produced the key with a trembling hand. Tears streamed down her face. Miss Lin, however, did not cry. She was looking into space with misty eyes, recalling that Kuomintang committeeman who had made a speech at her school, a hateful swarthy pockmarked fellow who stared at her like a hungry dog. She could picture him grasping the gold necklace and jumping for joy, his big mouth open in a laugh. Then she visualized the ugly bandit quarrelling with her father, hitting him....

"Aiya!" Miss Lin gave a frightened scream and threw herself on her mother's bosom. Mrs. Lin was so started she had no time for hiccups.

"Child, hic—don't cry," Mrs. Lin made a desperate effort to speak. "After New Year your Papa will have money. We'll make a new dress for you, hic— Those black-hearted crooks! They all insist we have money. Hic—we lose more every year. Your Papa was in the fertilizer business, and he lost money, hic— Every penny invested in the shop belongs to other people. Child, hic, hic—this sickness of mine; it makes life hell—hic—In another two years when you're nineteen, we'll find you a good husband. Hic—then I can die in peace! Save us from our adversity, Goddess Kuanyin! Hic—"

二

第二天,林先生的铺子里新换过一番布置。将近一星期不曾露脸的东洋货又都摆在最惹眼的地位了。林先生又摹仿上海大商店的办法,写了许多"大廉价照码九折"的红绿纸条,贴在玻璃窗上。这天是阴历腊月二十三,正是乡镇上洋广货店的"旺月"。不但林先生的额外支出"四百元"指望在这时候捞回来,就是林小姐的新衣服也靠托在这几天的生意好。

十点多钟,赶市的乡下人一群一群的在街上走过了,他们臂上挽着篮,或是牵着小孩子,粗声大气地一边在走,一边在谈话。他们望到了林先生的花花绿绿的铺面,都站住了,仰起脸,老婆唤丈夫,孩子叫爹娘,啧啧地夸羡那些货物。新年快到了,孩子们希望穿一双新袜子,女人们想到家里的面盆早就用破,全家合用的一条

II

The following day, Mr. Lin's shop underwent a transformation. All the Japanese goods he hadn't dared to show for the past week, now were the most prominently displayed. In imitation of the big Shanghai stores, Mr. Lin inscribed many slips of coloured paper with the words "Big Sale 10% Discount!" and pasted them on his windows. Just seven days before New Year, this was the "rush season" of the shops selling imported goods in the towns and villages. Not only was there hope of earning back Mr. Lin's special expenditure of four hundred dollars; Miss Lin's new dress depended on the amount of business done in the next few days.

A little past ten in the morning, group of peasants who had come into town to sell their produce in the market began drifting along the street. Carrying baskets on their arms, leading small children, they chatted loud and vigorously as they strolled. They stopped to look at the red and green blurbs pasted on Mr. Lin's windows and called attention to them, women shouting to their husbands, children yelling to their parents, clucking their tongues in admiration over the goods on display in the shop windows. It would soon be New Year. Children were wishing for a pair of new socks. Women remembered that the family wash-basin had been broken for some time. The single wash-cloth used

面巾还是半年前的老家伙,肥皂又断绝了一个多月,趁这里"卖贱货",正该买一点。林先生坐在账台上,抖擞着精神,堆起满脸的笑容,眼睛望着那些乡下人,又带睨着自己铺子里的两个伙计,两个学徒,满心希望货物出去,洋钱进来。但是这些乡下人看了一会,指指点点夸羡了一会,竟自懒洋洋地走到斜对门的裕昌祥铺面前站住了再看。林先生伸长了脖子,望到那班乡下人的背影,眼睛里冒出火来。他恨不得拉他们回来!

"呃——呃——"

坐在账台后面那道分隔铺面与"内宅"的蝴蝶门旁边的林大娘把勉强忍住了半晌的"呃"放出来。林小姐倚在她妈的身边,呆呆地望着街上不作声,心头却是卜卜地跳;她的新衣服至少已经走脱了半件。

林先生赶到柜台前睁大了妒忌的眼睛看着斜对门的同业裕昌祥。那边的四五个店员一字儿摆在柜台前,等候做买卖。但是那班乡下人没有一个走近到柜台边,他们看了一会儿,又

by the entire family had been bought half a year ago, and now was an old rag. They had run out of soap more than a month before. They ought to take advantage of this "Sale" and buy a few things.

Mr. Lin sat in the cashier's cage, marshalling all his energies, a broad smile plastered on his face. He watched the peasants, while keeping an eye on his two salesmen and two apprentices. With all his heart he hoped to see his merchandise start moving out and the silver dollars begin rolling in.

But these peasants, after looking a while, after pointing and gesticulating appreciatively a while, ambled over to the store across the street to stand and look some more. Craning his neck, Mr. Lin glared at the backs of the group of peasants, and sparks shot from his eyes. He wanted to go over and drag them back!

"Hic—hic—".

Behind the cashier's cage were swinging doors which separated the shop itself from the "inner sanctum." "Beside these doors sat Mrs. Lin releasing hiccups that she had long been suppressing with difficulty. Miss Lin was seated beside her. Entranced, the girl watched the street silently, her heart pounding. At least half of her new dress had just walked away.

Mr. Lin strode quickly to the front of the counter. He glared jealously at the shop opposite. Its five salesmen were waiting expectantly behind the counter. But not one peasant entered the store. They looked for a

19

照样的走过去了。林先生觉得心头一松,忍不住望着裕昌祥的伙计笑了一笑。这时又有七八人一队的乡下人走到林先生的铺面前,其中有一位年青的居然上前一步,歪着头看那些挂着的洋伞。林先生猛转过脸来,一对嘴唇皮立刻嘻开了;他亲自兜揽这位意想中的顾客了:

"喂,阿弟,买洋伞么?便宜货,一只洋卖九角!看看货色去。"

一个伙计已经取下了两三把洋伞,立刻撑开了一把,热刺刺地塞到那年青乡下人的手里,振起精神,使出夸卖的本领来:

"小当家,你看!洋缎面子,实心骨子,晴天,落雨,耐用好看!九角洋钱一顶,再便宜没有了!……那边是一只洋一顶,货色还没有这等好呢,你比一比就明白。"

那年青的乡下人拿着伞,没有主意似的张大了嘴巴。他回过头去望着一位五十多岁的老头子,又把手里的伞撅了一撅,似乎说:"买一把罢?"老头子却老大着急地吆喝道:

20

while, then continued on their way. Mr. Lin relaxed; he couldn't help grinning at the salesmen across the street. Another group of seven or eight peasants stopped before Mr. Lin's shop. A youngster among them actually came a step forward. With his head cocked to one side, he examined the imported umbrellas. Mr. Lin whirled around, his face breaking into a happy smile. He went to work personally on this prospective customer.

"Would you like a foreign umbrella, Brother? They're cheap. You only pay ninety cents on the dollar. Come and take a look."

A salesman had already taken down two or three imported umbrellas. He promptly opened one and shoved it earnestly into the young peasant's hand. Summoning all his zeal, the salesman launched into a high powered patter:

"Just look at this, young master! Foreign satin cloth, solid ribs. It's durable and handsome for rainy days or clear. Ninety cents each. They don't come any cheaper.... Across the street, they're a dollar apiece, but they're not as good as these. You can compare them and see why."

The young peasant held the umbrella and stood undecided, with his mouth open. He turned towards a man in his fifties and weighed the umbrella in his hand as if to ask "Shall I buy it?" The older man became very upset and began to shout at him.

"阿大！你昏了，想买伞！一船硬柴，一古脑儿只卖了三块多钱，你娘等着量米回去吃，哪有钱来买伞！"

"货色是便宜，没有钱买！"

站在那里观望的乡下人都叹着气说，懒洋洋地都走了。那年青的乡下人满脸涨红，摇一下头，放了伞也就要想走，这可把林先生急坏了，赶快让步问道：

"喂，喂，阿弟，你说多少钱呢？——再看看去，货色是靠得住的！"

"货色是便宜，钱不够。"

老头子一面回答，一面拉住了他的儿子，逃也似的走了。林先生苦着脸，踱回到账台里，浑身不得劲儿。他知道不是自己不会做生意，委实是乡下人太穷了，买不起九毛钱的一顶伞。他偷眼再望斜对门的裕昌祥，也还是只有人站在那里看，没有人上柜台买。裕昌祥左右邻的生泰杂货店万牲糕饼店那就简直连看的人都没有半个。一群一群走过的乡下人都挽着篮子，但篮子里空无一物；间或有花蓝布的一包儿，看样子就知道是米；甚至一个多月前乡下人收获的晚稻也早已被地主们和高利贷的债主们如数逼光，现在乡下人不得不一升两

"You're crazy! Buying an umbrella! We only got three dollars for the whole boatload of firewood, and your mother's waiting at home for us to bring back some rice. How can you spend money on an umbrella!"

"It's cheap, but we can't afford it!" sighed the peasants standing around watching. They walked slowly away. The young peasant, his face brick red, shook his head. He put down the umbrella and started to leave. Mr. Lin was frantic. He quickly gave ground.

"How much do you say, Brother? Take another look. It's fine merchandise!"

"It is cheap. But we don't have enough money," the older peasant replied, pulling his son. They practically ran away.

Bitterly, Mr. Lin returned to the cashier's cage, feeling weak all over. He knew it wasn't that he was an inept businessman. The peasants simply were too poor. They couldn't even spend ninety cents on an umbrella. He stole a glance at the shop across the way. There too people were looking, but no one was going in. In front of the neighbouring grocery store and the cookie shop, no one was even looking. Group after group of the country folk walked by carrying baskets. But the baskets all were empty. Occasionally, someone appeared with a homespun flowered blue cloth sack, filled with rice, from the look of it. The late rice which the peasants had harvested more than a month before had long since been squeezed out as rent for the landlords and interest

升的量着贵米吃。这一切,林先生都明白,他就觉得自己的一份生意至少是间接的被地主和高利贷者剥夺去了。

时间渐渐移近正午,街上走的乡下人已经很少了,林先生的铺子就只做成了一块多钱的生意,仅仅足够开销了"大廉价照码九折"的红绿纸条的广告费。林先生垂头丧气走进"内宅"去,几乎没有勇气和女儿老婆相见。林小姐含着一泡眼泪,低着头坐在屋角;林大娘在一连串的打呃中,挣扎着对丈夫说:

"花了四百块钱,——又忙了一个晚上摆设起来,呃,东洋货是准卖了,却又生意清淡,呃——阿囡的爷呀!……吴妈又要拿工钱——"

"还只半天呢! 不要着急。"

林先生勉强安慰着,心里的难受,比刀割还厉害。他闷闷地踱了几步。所有推广营业的方法都想遍了,觉得都不是

for the usurers. Now in order to have rice to eat, the peasants were forced to buy a measure or two at a time, at steep prices

All this Mr. Lin knew. He felt that at least part of his business was being indirectly eaten away by the usurers and landlords.

The hour gradually neared noon. There were very few peasants on the street now. Mr. Lin's shop had done a little over one dollar's worth of business, just enough to cover the cost of the "Big Sale 10% Discount" strips of red and green paper. Despondently, Mr. Lin entered the "inner sanctum." He barely had the courage to face his wife and daughter. Miss Lin's eyes were filled with tears. She sat in the corner with her head down. Mrs. Lin was in the middle of a string of hiccups. Struggling for control, she addressed her husband.

"We laid out four hundred dollars—and spent all night getting things ready in the shop—hic! We got permission to sell the Japanese goods, but business is dead—hic—my blessed ancestors!... The maid wants her wages—"

"It's only half a day. Don't worry." Mr. Lin forced a comforting note into his voice, but he felt worse than if a knife were cutting through his heart. Gloomily, he paced back and forth. He thought of all the business promotion tricks he knew, but none of

林家铺子

路。生意清淡,早已各业如此,并不是他一家呀;人们都穷了,可没有法子。但是他总还希望下午的营业能够比较好些。本镇的人家买东西大概在下午。难道他们过新年不买些东西?只要他们存心买,林先生的营业是有把握的。毕竟他的货物比别家便宜。

是这盼望使得林先生依然能够抖擞着精神坐在账台上守候他意想中的下午的顾客。

这下午照例和上午显然不同:街上并没很多的人,但几乎每个人都相识,都能够叫出他们的姓名,或是他们的父亲和祖父的姓名。林先生靠在柜台上,用了异常温和的眼光迎送这些慢慢地走着谈着经过他那铺面的本镇人。他时常笑嘻嘻地迎着常有交易的人喊道:

"呵,××哥,到清风阁去吃茶么?小店大放盘,交易点儿去!"

有时被唤着的那位居然站住了,走上柜台来,于是林先生和他的店员就要大忙而特忙,异常敏感地伺察着这位未可知的顾客的眼光,瞧见他的眼光

them seemed any good. Business was bad. It had been bad in all lines for some time; his shop wasn't the only one having difficulty. People were poor, and there wasn't anything that could be done about it. Still, he hoped business would be better in the afternoon. The local townspeople usually did their buying then. Surely they would buy things for New Year! If only they wanted to buy, Mr. Lin's shop was certain of trade. After all, his merchandise was cheaper than other shops!

It was this hope that enabled Mr. Lin to bolster his sagging spirits as he sat in the cashier's cage awaiting the customers he pictured coming in the afternoon.

And the afternoon proved to be different indeed from the morning. There weren't many people on the street, but Mr. Lin knew nearly every one of them. He knew their names, or the names of their fathers or grandfathers. These were local townspeople, and as they chatted and walked slowly past his shop, Mr. Lin's eyes, glowing with cordiality, welcomed them, and sent them on their way. At times, with a broad smile he greeted an old customer.

"Ah, Brother, going out to the tea-house? Our little shop has slashed its prices. Favour us with a small purchase!"

Sometimes, the man would actually stop and come into the shop. Then Mr. Lin and his assistants would plunge into a frenzy of activity. With acute sensitiveness, they would watch the eyes of the unpredictable

瞥到什么货物上，就赶快拿出那种货物请他考较。林小姐站在那对蝴蝶门边看望，也常常被林先生唤出来对那位未可知的顾客叫一声"伯伯"。小学徒送上一杯便茶来，外加一枝小联珠。

在价目上，林先生也格外让步；遇到那位顾客一定要除去一毛钱左右尾数的时候，他就从店员手里拿过那算盘来算了一会儿，然后不得已似的把那尾数从算盘上拨去，一面笑嘻嘻地说：

"真不够本呢！可是老主顾，只好遵命了。请你多作成几笔生意罢！"

整个下午就是这么张罗着过去了。连现带赊，大大小小，居然也有十来注交易。林先生早已汗透棉袍。虽然是累得那么着，林先生心里却很愉快。他冷眼偷看斜对门的裕昌祥，似乎赶不上自己铺子的"热闹"。常在那对蝴蝶门旁边看望的林小姐脸上也有些笑意，

customer. The moment his eyes rested on a piece of merchandise, the salesmen would swiftly produce one just like it and invite the customer to examine it. Miss Lin watched from beside the swinging doors, and her father frequently called her out to respectfully greet the unpredictable customer as "Uncle." An apprentice would serve him a glass of tea and offer him a good cigarette.

On the question of price, Mr. Lin was exceptionally flexible. When a customer was firm about knocking off a few odd cents from the round figure of his purchase price, Mr. Lin would take the abacus from the hands of his salesman and calculate personally. Then, with the air of a man who has been driven to the wall, he would deduct the few odd cents from the total bill.

"We'll take a loss on this sale," he would say with a wry smile. "But you're an old customer. We have to please you. Come and buy some more things soon!"

The entire afternoon was spent in this manner. Including cash and credit, big purchases and small, the shop made a total of over ten sales. Mr. Lin was drenched with perspiration, and although he was worn out, he was very happy. He had been sneaking looks at the shop across the street. They didn't seem to be nearly so busy. There was a pleased expression on the face of Miss Lin, who had been constantly watching from beside the swinging doors. Mrs. Lin even jerked

林大娘也少打几个呃了。

　　快到上灯时候,林先生核算这一天的"流水账";上午等于零,下午卖了十六元八角五分,八块钱是赊账。林先生微微一笑,但立即皱紧了眉头了;他今天的"大放盘"确是照本出卖,开销都没着落,官利更说不上。他呆了一会儿,又开了账箱,取出几本账簿来翻着打了半天算盘;账上"人欠"的数目共有一千三百余元,本镇六百多,四乡七百多;可是"欠人"的客账,单是上海的东升字号就有八百,合计不下二千哪!林先生低声叹一口气,觉得明天以后如果生意依然没见好,那他这年关就有点难过了。他望着玻璃窗上"大放盘照码九折"的红绿纸条,心里这么想:"照今天那样当真放盘,生意总该会见好;亏本么? 没有生意也是照样的要开销。只好先拉些主顾来再慢慢儿想法提高货码

out a few less hiccups.

Shortly before dark, Mr. Lin finished adding up his accounts for the day. The morning amounted to zero; in the afternoon they had sold sixteen dollars and eighty-five cents worth of merchandise, eight dollars of it being on credit. Mr. Lin smiled sligtly, then he frowned. He had been selling all his goods at their original cost. He hadn't even covered his expenses for the day, to say nothing of making any profit. His mind was blank for a moment. Then he took out his account books and calculated in them for a long time. On the "credit" side there was a total of over thirteen hundred dollars of uncollected debts—more than six hundred in town and over seven hundred in the countryside. But the "debit" ledger showed a figure of eight hundred dollars owed to the big Shanghai wholesale house alone. He owed a total of not less than two thousand dollars!

Mr. Lin sighed softly. If business continued to be so bad, it was going to be a little difficult for him to get through New Year. He looked at the red and green paper slips on the window announcing "Big Sale 10% Discount." If we really cut prices like we did today, business ought to pick up, he thought to himself. We're not making any profit, but if we don't do any business I still have to pay expenses anyway. The main thing is to get the customers to come in, then I can gradually raise my prices.... If we can do some whole-

……要是四乡还有批发生意来,那就更好!——"

突然有一个人来打断林先生的甜蜜梦想了。这是五十多岁的一位老婆子,巍颤颤地走进店来,手里拿着一个小小的蓝布包。林先生猛抬起头来,正和那老婆子打一个照面,想躲避也躲避不及,只好走上前去招呼她道:

"朱三太,出来买过年东西么?请到里面去坐坐。——阿秀,来扶朱三太。"

林小姐早已不在那对蝴蝶门边了,没有听到。那朱三太连连摇手,就在铺面里的一张椅子上坐了,郑重地打开她的蓝布手巾包,——包里仅有一扣折子,她抖抖簌簌地双手捧了,直送到林先生的鼻子前,她的瘪嘴唇扭了几扭,正想说话,林先生早已一手接过那折子,同时抢先说道;

"我晓得了。明天送到你府上罢。"

"哦,哦;十月,十一月,十二月,一总是三个月,三三得九,是九块罢?——明天你送来?哦,哦,不要送,让我带了去。嗯!"

朱三太扭着她的瘪嘴唇,很艰难似的说。她有三百元的

sale business in the countryside, that will be even better!...

Suddenly, someone broke in on Mr. Lin's sweet dream. A shaky old lady entered the shop carrying a little bundle wrapped in blue cloth. Mr. Lin yanked up his head to find her confronting him. He wanted to escape, but there was no time. He could only go forward and greet her.

"Ah, Mrs. Zhu, out buying things for the New Year? Please come into the back room and sit down.—Xiu, give Mrs. Chu your arm."

But Miss Lin didn't hear. She had left the swinging doors some time ago. Mrs. Zhu waved her hand in refusal and sat down on a chair in the store. Solemnly, she unwrapped the blue cloth and brought out a small account book. With two trembling hands she presented the book under Mr. Lin's nose. Twisting her withered lips, she was about to speak, but Mr. Lin had already taken the book and was hastening to say:

"I understand, I'll send it to your house tomorrow."

"Mm, mm, the tenth month, the eleventh month, the twelfth month; altogether three months. Three threes are nine; that's nine dollars, isn't it? —you'll send the money tomorrow? Mm, mm, you don't have to send it. I'll take it back with me! Eh!"

The words seemed to come with difficulty from Mrs. Zhu's withered mouth. She had three hundred

"老本"存在林先生的铺里,按月来取三块钱的利息,可是最近林先生却拖欠了三个月,原说是到了年底总付,明天是送灶日,老婆子要买送灶的东西,所以亲自上林先生的铺子来了。看她那股扭起了一对瘪嘴唇的劲儿,光景是钱不到手就一定不肯走。

林先生抓着头皮不作声。这九块钱的利息,他何尝存心白赖,只是三个月来生意清淡,每天卖得的钱仅够开伙食,付捐税,不知不觉就拖欠下来了。然而今天要是不付,这老婆子也许会就在铺面上嚷闹,那就太丢脸,对于营业的前途很有影响。

"好,好,带了去罢,带了去罢!"

林先生终于斗气似的说,声音有点儿梗咽。他跑到账台里,把上下午卖得的现钱归并起来,又从腰包里掏出一个双毫,这才凑成了八块大洋,十角小洋,四十个铜子,交付了朱三太。当他看见那老婆子把这些银洋铜子郑重地数了又数,而且抖抖簌簌地放在那蓝布手巾上包了起来的时候,他忍不住叹一口气,异想天开地打算拉

dollars loaned to Mr. Lin's shop, and was entitled to three dollars interest every month. Mr. Lin had delayed payment for three months, promising to pay in full at the end of the year. Now, she needed some money to buy gifts for tomorrow's Kitchen God Festival, and so she had come seeking Mr. Lin. From the forcefulness with which she moved her puckered mouth, Mr. Lin could tell that she was determined not to leave without the money.

Mr. Lin scratched his head in silence. He hadn't been deliberately refusing to pay the interest. It was just that for the past three months business had been poor. Their daily sales had been barely enough to cover their food and taxes. He had delayed paying her unconsciously. But if he didn't pay her today, the old lady might raise a row in the shop. That would be too shameful and would seriously influence the shop's future.

"All right, all right. Take it back with you!" Mr. Lin finally said in exasperation. His voice shook a little. He rushed to the cashier's cage and gathered together all the cash that had been taken in that morning and afternoon. To that he added twenty cents from his own pocket, and presented the whole collection of dollars, pennies and dimes to the old lady. She carefully counted the lot over and over again, then with trembling hands wrapped the money in the blue cloth. Mr. Lin couldn't repress a sigh. He had a wild desire to

35

回几文来;他勉强笑着说:

"三阿太,你这蓝布手巾太旧了,买一块老牌麻纱白手帕去罢?我们有上好的洗脸手巾,肥皂,买一点儿去新年里用罢。价钱公道!"

"不要,不要;老太婆了,用不到。"

朱三太连连摇手说,把折子藏在衣袋里,捧着她的蓝布手巾包竟自去了。

林先生哭丧着脸,走回"内宅"去。因这朱三太的上门讨利息,他记起还有两注存款,桥头陈老七的二百元和张寡妇的一百五十元,总共十来块钱的利息,都是"不便"拖欠的,总得先期送去。他抡着指头算日子:二十四,二十五,二十六——到二十六,放在四乡的账头该可以收齐了,店里的寿生是前天出去收账的,极迟是二十六应该回来了;本镇的账头总得到二十八九方才有个数目。然而上海号家的收账客人说不定明后天就会到,只有再向恒源钱庄去借了。但是明天

snatch back a part of the cash.

"That blue handkerchief is too worn, Mrs. Zhu," he said with a forced laugh. "Why not buy a good white linen one? We've also got top quality wash-cloths and soap. Take some to use over the New Year. Prices are reasonable!"

"No, I don't want any. An old lady like me doesn't need that kind of thing." She waved her hand in refusal. She put her account book in her pocket and departed, firmly grasping the blue cloth bundle.

Looking sour, Mr. Lin walked into the "inner sanctum."Mrs. Zhu's visit reminded him that he had two other creditors. Old Chen and Widow Zhang had put up two hundred and one hundred and fifty dollars respectively. He would have to pay them a total of ten dollars interest. He couldn't very well delay their money; in fact, he would have to pay them ahead of time. He counted on his fingers—twenty-fourth, twenty-fifth, twenty-sixth. By the twenty-sixth, he ought to be able to collect all the outstanding debts in the countryside. His clerk Shousheng had gone off on a collection trip the day before yesterday. He should be back by the twenty-sixth at the latest. The unpaid bills in town couldn't be collected till the twenty-eighth or twenty-ninth. But the collector from the Shanghai wholesale house to which Mr. Lin owed money would probably come tomorrow or the day after. Lin's only alternative was to borrow more from the local bank. And how

的门市怎样？……

他这么低着头一边走，一边想，猛听得女儿的声音在他耳边说：

"爸爸，你看这块大绸好么？七尺，四块二角，不贵罢？"

林先生心里蓦地一跳，站住了睁大着眼睛，说不出话。林小姐手里托着那块绸，却在那里憨笑。四块二角！数目可真不算大，然而今天店里总共只卖得十六块多，并且是老实照本贱卖的呀！林先生怔了一会儿，这才没精打彩地问道：

"你哪来的钱呢？"

"挂在账上。"

林先生听得又是欠账，忍不住皱一下眉头。但女儿是自己宠惯了的，林大娘又抵死偏护着，林先生没奈何只有苦笑。过一会儿，他叹一口气，轻轻埋怨道：

"那么性急！过了年再买岂不是好！"

三

又过了两天，"大放盘"的林先生的铺子，生意果然很好，每天可以做三十多元的生意了。林大娘的打呃，大大减少，平均是五分钟来一次；林小姐

would business be tomorrow?...

His head down, Mr. Lin paced back and forth, thinking. The voice of his daughter spoke into his ear:

"Papa, what do you think of this piece of silk? Four dollars and twenty cents for seven feet. That's not expensive, is it?"

Mr. Lin's heart gave a leap. He stood stock-still and glared, speechless. Miss Lin held the piece of silk in her hand and giggled. Four dollars and twenty cents! It wasn't a big sum, but the shop only did sixteen dollars worth of business all day, and really at cost price! Mr. Lin stood frozen, then asked weakly:

"Where did you get the money?"

"I put it on the books."

Another debit. Mr. Lin scowled. But he had spoiled his daughter himself, and Mrs. Lin would take the girl's side no matter what the case might be. He smiled a helpless bitter smile. Then he sighed.

"You're always in such a rush," he said, slightly reproving. "Why couldn't you wait till after New Year!"

III

Another two days went by. Business was indeed very brisk in Mr. Lin's shop, with its "Big Sale." They did over thirty dollars in sales every day. The hiccups of Mrs. Lin diminished considerably; she hiccuped on the average of only once every five minutes.

在铺面和"内宅"之间跳进跳出,脸上红喷喷地时常在笑,有时竟在铺面帮忙招呼生意,直到林大娘再三唤她,方才跑进去,一边擦着额上的汗珠,一边兴冲冲地急口说:

"妈呀,又叫我进来干么!我不觉得辛苦呀!妈!爸爸累得满身是汗,嗓子也喊哑了!——刚才一个客人买了五块钱东西呢!妈!不要怕我辛苦,不要怕!爸爸叫我歇一会儿就出去呢!"

林大娘只是点头,打一个呃,就念一声"大慈大悲菩萨"。客厅里本就供奉着一尊瓷观音,点着一炷香,林大娘就摇摇摆摆走过去磕头,谢菩萨的保佑,还要祷告菩萨一发慈悲,保佑林先生的生意永远那么好,保佑林小姐易长易大,明年就得个好女婿。

但是在铺面张罗的林先生虽然打起精神做生意,脸上笑容不断,心里却像有几根线牵着。每逢卖得了一块钱,看见顾客欣然挟着纸包而去,林先生就忍不住心里一顿,在他心里的算盘上就加添了五分洋钱

Miss Lin skipped up and back between the shop and the "inner sanctum," her face flushed and smiling. At times she even helped with the selling. Only after her mother called her repeatedly, did she return to the back room. Mopping her brow, she protested excitedly.

"Ma, why have you called me back again? It's not hard work! Ma, Papa's so tired he's soaking wet; his voice is gone! — A customer just made a five-dollar purchase! Ma, you don't have to be afraid it's too tiring for me! Don't worry! Papa told me to rest a while, then come out again!"

Mrs. Lin only nodded her head and hiccuped, followed by a murmur that "Buddha is merciful and kind." A porcelain image of the Goddess Kuanyin was enshrined in the "inner sanctum," with a stick of incense burning before it. Mrs. Lin swayed over to the shrine and kowtowed. She thanked the Goddess for Her Protection and prayed for Her Blessing on a number of matters—that Mr. Lin's business should always be good, that Miss Lin should grow nicely, that next year the girl should get a good husband.

But out in the shop, although Mr. Lin was devoting his whole being to business, though a smile never left his face, he felt as if his heart were bound with strings. Watching the satisfied customer going out with a package under his arm, Mr. Lin suffered a pang with every dollar he took in, as the abacus in his mind clicked a five per cent loss off the cost price he had

的血本的亏折。他几次想把这个"大放盘"时每块钱的实足亏折算成三分,可是无论如何,算来算去总得五分。生意虽然好,他却越卖越心疼了。在柜台上招呼主顾的时候,他这种矛盾的心理有时竟至几乎使他发晕。偶尔他偷眼望望斜对门的裕昌祥,就觉得那边闲立在柜台边的店员和掌柜,嘴角上都带着讥讽的讪笑,似乎都在说:"看这姓林的傻子呀,当真亏本放盘哪!看着罢,他的生意越好,就越亏本,倒闭得越快!"那时候,林先生便咬一下嘴唇,决定明天无论如何要把货码提高,要把次等货标上头等货的价格。

给林先生斡旋那"封存东洋货"问题的商会长当走过林家铺子的时候,也微微笑着,站住了对林先生贺喜,并且拍着林先生的肩膀,轻声说:

"如何?四百块钱是花得不冤枉罢!——可是,卜局长那边,你也得稍稍点缀,防他看得眼红,也要来敲诈。生意好,妒忌的人就多;就是卜局长不生心,他们也要去挑拨呀!"

raised through sweat and blood. Several times he tried to estimate the loss as being three per cent, but no matter how he figured it, he still was losing five cents on the dollar. Although business was good, the more he sold the worse he felt. As he waited on the customers, the conflict raging within his breast at times made him nearly faint. When he stole glances at the shop across the street, he had the impression that the owner and salesmen were sneering at him from behind their counters. Look at that fool Lin! they seemed to be saying. He really *is* selling below cost! Wait and see! The more business he does, the more he loses! The sooner he'll have to close down!

Mr. Lin gnawed his lips. He vowed he would raise his prices the next day. He would charge first-grade prices for second-rate merchandise.

The head of the Merchants Guild came by. It was he who had interceded with the Kuomintang chieftains for Mr. Lin on the question of selling Japanese goods. Now he smiled and congratulated Mr. Lin, and clapped him on the shoulder.

"How goes it? That four hundred dollars was well spent!" he said softly. "But you'd better give a small token to Kuomintang Party Commissioner Pu too. Otherwise, he may become annoyed and try to squeeze you. When business is good, plenty of people are jealous. Even if Commissioner Pu doesn't have any 'ideas,' they'll try to stir him up!"

林先生谢商会长的关切,心里老大吃惊,几乎连做生意都没有精神。

然而最使他心神不宁的,是店里的寿生出去收账到现在还没有回来,林先生是等着寿生收的钱来开销"客账"。上海东升字号的收账客人前天早已到镇,直催逼得林先生再没有话语文吾了。如果寿生再不来,林先生只有向恒源钱庄借款的一法,这一来,林先生又将多负担五六十元的利息,这在见天亏本的林先生委实比割肉还心疼。

到四点钟光景,林先生忽然听得街上走过的人们乱哄哄地在议论着什么,人们的脸色都很惶急,似乎发生了什么大事情了。一心惦念着出去收账的寿生是否平安的林先生就以为一定是快班船遭了强盗抢,他的心卜卜地乱跳。他唤住了一个路人焦急地问道:

"什么事?是不是栗市快班遭了强盗抢?"

"哦!又是强盗抢么?路上真不太平!抢,还是小事,还要绑人去哪!"

那人,有名的闲汉陆和尚,含糊地回答,同时睒着半只眼

Mr. Lin thanked the head of the Merchants Guild for his concern. Inwardly, he was very alarmed. He almost lost his zest for doing business.

What made him most uneasy was that his assistant Shousheng still hadn't returned from the bill collecting trip. He needed the money to pay off his account with the big Shanghai wholesale house. The collector had arrived from Shanghai two days before, and was pressing Mr. Lin hard. If Shousheng didn't come soon, Mr. Lin would have to borrow from the local bank. This would mean an additional burden of fifty or sixty dollars in interest payments. To Mr. Lin, losing money every day, this prospect was more painful than being flayed alive.

At about four p.m., Mr. Lin suddenly heard a noisy uproar on the street. People looked very frightened, as though some serious calamity had happened. Mr. Lin, who could think only of whether Shousheng would safely return, was sure that the river boat on which Shousheng would come back had been set upon by pirates. His heart pounding, he hailed a passer-by and asked worriedly:

"What's wrong? Did pirates get the boat from Lishi?"

"Oh! So it's pirates again? Travelling is really too dangerous! Robbing is nothing. Men are even kindnapped right off the boat!" babbled the passer-by, a well-known loafer named Lu. He eyed the brightly co-

睛看林先生铺子里花花绿绿的货物。林先生不得要领,心里更急,丢开陆和尚,就去问第二个走近来的人,桥头的王三毛。

"听说栗市班遭抢,当真么?"

"那一定是太保阿书手下人干的,太保阿书是枪毙了,他的手下人多么厉害!"

王三毛一边回答,一边只顾走。可是林先生却急坏了,冷汗从额角上钻出来。他早就估量到寿生一定是今天回来,而且是从栗市——收账程序中预定的最后一处,坐快班船回来;此刻已是四点钟,不见他来,王三毛又是那样说,那还有什么疑义么?林先生竟忘记了这所谓"栗市班遭强盗抢"乃是自己的发明了!他满脸急汗,直往"内宅"跑;在那对蝴蝶门边忘记跨门槛,几乎绊了一交。

"爸爸!上海打仗了!东洋兵放炸弹烧闸北——"

林小姐大叫着跑到林先生跟前。

林先生怔了一下。什么上海打仗,原就和他不相干,但中间既然牵连着"东洋兵",又好像不能不追问一声了。他看着女儿的很兴奋的脸孔问道:

loured goods in the shop.

Mr. Lin could make no sense out of this at all. His worry increased and he dropped Lu to accost Wang, the next person who came along.

"Is it true that the boat from Lishi was robbed?"

"It must be Ah Shu's gang that did it. Ah Shu has been shot, but his gang is still a tough bunch!" Wang replied without slackening his pace.

Cold sweat bedewed Mr. Lin's forehead. He was frantic. He was sure that Shou-sheng was coming back today, and from Lishi. That was the last place on the account book list. Now it was already four o'clock, but there was no sign of Shousheng. After what Wang had said, how could Mr. Lin have any doubts? He forgot that he himself had invented the story of the boat being robbed. His whole face beaded with perspiration, he rushed into the "inner sanctum." Going through the swinging doors, he tripped over the threshold and nearly fell.

"Papa, they're fighting in Shanghai! The Japanese bombed the Zhabei section!" cried Miss Lin, running up to him.

Mr. Lin stopped short. What was all this about fighting in Shanghai? His first reaction was that it had nothing to do with him. But since it involved the "Japanese," he thought he had better inquire a little further. Looking at his daughter's agitated face, he asked:

47

"东洋兵放炸弹么?你从哪里听来的?"

"街上走过的人全是那么说。东洋兵放大炮,掷炸弹。闸北烧光了!"

"哦,那么,有人说栗市快班强盗抢么?"

林小姐摇头,就像扑火的灯蛾似的扑向外面去了。林先生迟疑了一会儿,站在那蝴蝶门边抓头皮。林大娘在里面打呃,又是喃喃地祷告:"菩萨保佑,炸弹不要落到我们头上来!"林先生转身再到铺子里,却见女儿和两个店员正在谈得很热闹。对门生泰杂货店里的老板金老虎也站在柜台外边指手划脚地讲谈。上海打仗,东洋飞机掷炸弹烧了闸北,上海已经罢市,全都证实了。强盗抢快班船么?没有听人说起过呀!栗市快班么?早已到了,一路平安。金老虎看见那快班船上的伙计刚刚背着两个蒲包走过的。林先生心里松一口气,知道寿生今天又没回来,但也知道好好儿的没有逢到强盗抢。

现在是满街都在议论上海的战事了。小伙计们夹在闹里

"The Japanese bombed it? Who told you that?"

"Everyone on the street is talking about it. The Japanese soldiers fired heavy artillery and they bombed. Zhabei is burned to the ground!"

"Oh, well, did anyone say that the boat from Lishi was robbed?"

Miss Lin shook her head, then fluttered from the room like a moth. Mr. Lin hesitated beside the swinging doors, scratching his head. Mrs. Lin was hiccuping and mumbling prayers.

"Buddha protect us! Don't let any bombs fall on our heads!"

Mr. Lin turned and went out to the shop. He saw his daughter engaged in excited conversation with the two salesmen. The owner of the shop across the street had come out from behind his counter and was talking, gesticulating wildly. There was fighting in Shanghai; Japanese planes had bombed Zhabei and burned it; the merchants in Shanghai had closed down—it all was true. What about the pirates robbing the boat? No one had heard anything about that! And the boat from Lishi? It had come in safely. The shopowner across the street had just seen stevedores from the boat going by with two big crates. Mr. Lin was relieved. Shousheng hadn't come back today, but he hadn't been robbed by pirates either!

Now the whole town was talking about the catastrophe in Shanghai. Young clerks were cursing the Jap-

骂"东洋乌龟!"竟也有人当街大呼:"再买东洋货就是忘八!"林小姐听着,脸上就飞红了一大片。林先生却还不动神色。大家都卖东洋货,并且大家花了几百块钱以后,都已经奉着特许:"只要把东洋商标撕去了就行。"他现在满店的货物都已经称为"国货",买主们也都是"国货,国货"地说着,就拿走了。在此满街人人为了上海的战事而没有心思想到生意的时候,林先生始终在筹虑他的正事。他还是不肯花重利去借庄款,他去和上海号家的收账客人情商,请他再多等这么一天两天。他的寿生极迟明天傍晚总该会到。

"林老板,你也是明白人,怎么说出这种话来呀!现在上海开了火,说不定明后天火车就不通,我是巴不得今晚上就动身呢!怎么再等一两天?请你今天把账款缴清,明天一早我好走。我也是吃人家的饭,请你照顾照顾罢!"

anese aggressors. People were even shouting, "Anyone who buys Japanese goods is a son of a bitch!" These words brought a scarlet blush to Miss Lin's cheeks, but Mr. Lin showed no change of expression. All the shops were selling Japanese merchandise. Moreover, after spending a few hundred dollars, the merchants had received special authorizations from the Kuomintang chieftains, saying, "The goods may be sold after removing the Japanese markings." All the merchandise in Mr. Lin's shop had been transformed into "native goods." His customers, too, would call them "native goods," then take up their packages and leave.

Because of the war in Shanghai, the whole town had lost all interest in business, but Mr. Lin was busy pondering his affairs. Unwilling to borrow from the local bank at exorbitant interest, he sought out the collector from the Shanghai wholesale house, to plead with him as a friend for a delay of another day or two. Shousheng would be back tomorrow before dark at the latest, said Mr. Lin. Then he would pay in full.

"My dear Mr. Lin, you're an intelligent man. How can you talk like that? They're fighting in Shanghai. Train service may be cut off tomorrow or the day after. I only wish I could start back tonight! How can I wait a day or two? Please, settle your account today so that I can leave the first thing tomorrow morning. I'm not my own boss. Please have some consideration for me!"

上海客人毫无通融地拒绝了林先生的情商。林先生看来是无可商量了，只好忍痛去到恒源钱庄上商借。他还恐怕那"钱猢狲"知道他是急用，要趁火打劫，高抬利息。谁知钱庄经理的口气却完全不对了。那痨病鬼经理听完了林先生的申请，并没作答，只管捧着他那老古董的水烟筒卜落落卜落落的呼，直到烧完一根纸吹，这才慢吞吞地说：

"不行了！东洋兵开仗，上海罢市，银行钱庄都封关，知道他们几时弄得好！上海这路一断，敝庄就成了没脚蟹，汇划不通，比尊处再好的户头也只好不做了。对不起，实在爱莫能助！"

林先生呆了一呆，还总以为这痨病鬼经理故意刁难，无非是为提高利息作地步，正想结结实实说几句恳求的话，却不料那经理又逼进一步道：

"刚才敝东吩咐过，他得的信，这次的乱子恐怕要闹大，叫我们收紧盘子！尊处原欠五

The Shanghai collector was uncompromisingly firm in his refusal. Mr. Lin saw that it was hopeless; he had no choice but to bear the pain and seek a loan from the local banker. He was worried that "Old Miser" knew of his sore need and would take advantage of the situation to boost the interest rate. From the minute he started speaking to the bank manager, Mr. Lin could feel that the atmosphere was all wrong. The tubercular old man said nothing when Mr. Lin finished his plea, but continued puffing on his antique water-pipe. After the whole packet of tobacco was consumed, the manager finally spoke.

"I can't do it," he said slowly. "The Japanese have begun fighting, business in Shanghai is at a standstill, the banks have all closed down—who knows when things will be set right again! Cut off from Shanghai, my bank is like a crab without legs. With exchange of remittances stopped, I couldn't do business even with a better client than you. I'm sorry. I'd love to help you but my hands are tied!"

Mr. Lin lingered. He thought the tubercular manager was putting on an act in preparation for demanding higher interest. Just as Mr. Lin was about to play along by renewing his pleas, he was surprised to hear the manager press him a step farther.

"Our employer has given us instructions. He has heard that the situation will probably get worse. He wants us to tighten up. Your shop originally owed us

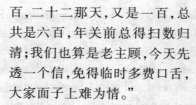

百,二十二那天,又是一百,总共是六百,年关前总得扫数归清;我们也算是老主顾,今天先透一个信,免得临时多费口舌,大家面子上难为情。"

"哦——可是小店里也实在为难。要看账头收得怎样。"

林先生呆了半晌,这才呐出这两句话。

"嘿!何必客气!宝号里这几天来的生意比众不同,区区六百块钱,还为难么?今天是同老兄说明白了,总望扫数归清,我在敝东跟前好交代。"

痨病鬼经理冷冷地说,站起来了。林先生冷了半截身子,瞧情形是万难挽回,只好硬着头皮走出了那家钱庄。他此时这才明白原来远在上海的打仗也要影响到他的小铺子了。今年的年关当真是难过:上海的收账客人立逼着要钱,恒源里不许宕过年,寿生还没回来,知道他怎样了,镇上的账头,去年只收起八成,今年瞧来连八

five hundred; on the twentysecond, you borrowed another hundred—altogether six hundred, due to be settled before New Year. We've been doing business together a long time, so I'm tipping you off. We want to avoid a lot off talk and embarrassment at the last minute."

"Oh—but our little shop is having a hard time," blurted the dumbfounded Mr. Lin. "I'll have to see how we do with our collections."

"Ho! Why be so modest! The last few days your business hasn't been like the others! What's so difficult about paying a mere six hundred dollars? I'm letting you know today, old brother. I'm looking forward to your settling your debt so that I can clear myself with my employer."

The tubercular manager spoke coldly. He stood up. Chilled, Mr. Lin could see that the situation was beyond repair. All he could do was to take a grip on himself and walk out of the bank. At last he understood that the fighting in distant Shanghai would influence his little shop too. It certainly was going to be hard to get through this New Year: The Shanghai collector was pressing him for money; the bank wouldn't wait until after the New Year; Shousheng still hadn't come back and there was no telling how he was getting on. So far as Mr. Lin's outstanding accounts in town were concerned, last year he had only collected eighty per cent. From the looks of things, this year there was no guar-

成都捏不稳——横在他前面的路,只是一条:"暂停营业,清理账目!"而这条路也就等于破产,他这铺子里早已没有自己的资本,一旦清理,剩给他的,光景只有一家三口三个光身子!

林先生愈想愈仄,走过那座望仙桥时,他看着桥下的浑水,几乎想纵身一跳完事。可是有一个人在背后唤他道:

"林先生,上海打仗了,是真的罢?听说东栅外刚刚调来了一枝兵,到商会里要借饷,开口就是二万,商会里正在开会呢!"

林先生急回过脸去看,原来正是那位存有两百块钱在他铺子里的陈老七,也是林先生的一位债主。

"哦——"

林先生打一个冷噤,只回答了这一声,就赶快下桥,一口气跑回家去。

四

这晚上的夜饭,林大娘在家常的一荤二素以外,特又添

antee of even that much. Only one road seemed open to Mr. Lin: "Business Temporarily Closed—Balancing Books!" And this was equivalent to bankruptcy. There hadn't been any of his own money invested in the shop for a long time. The day the books were balanced and the creditors paid off, what would be left for him probably wouldn't be enough to stand between his family and nakedness!

The more he thought, the worse Mr. Lin felt. Crossing the bridge, he looked at the turbid water below. He was almost tempted to jump and end it all. Then a man hailed him from behind.

"Mr. Lin, is it true there's a war on in Shanghai? I hear that a bunch of soldiers just set up outside the town's east gate and asked the Merchants Guild for a 'loan.' They wanted twenty thousand right off the bat. The Merchants Guild is holding a meeting about it now!"

Mr. Lin hurriedly turned around. The speaker was Old Chen who had two hundred dollars loaned to the shop—another of Mr. Lin's creditors.

"Oh—" retorted Mr. Lin with a shiver. Quickly he crossed the bridge and ran home.

IV

For dinner that evening, beside the usual one meat dish and two vegetable dishes, Mrs. Lin had

了一个碟子,是到八仙楼买来的红焖肉,林先生心爱的东西。另外又有一斤黄酒。林小姐笑不离口,为的铺子里生意好,为的大绸新旗袍已经做成,也为的上海竟然开火,打东洋人。林大娘打呃的次数更加少了,差不多十分钟只来一回。

只有林先生心里发闷到要死。他喝着闷酒,看看女儿,又看看老婆,几次想把那炸弹似的恶消息宣布,然而终于没有那样的勇气。并且他还不曾绝望,还想挣扎,至少是还想掩饰他的两下里碰不到头。所以当商会里议决了答应借饷五千并且要林先生摊认二十元的时候,他毫不推托,就答应下来了。他决定非到最后五分钟不让老婆和女儿知道那家道困难的真实情形。他的划算是这样的:人家欠他的账收一个八成罢,他还人家的账也是个八成,——反正可以借口上海打仗,钱庄不通;为难的是人欠我欠之间尚差六百光景,那只有用剜肉补疮的方法拼命放盘卖贱货,且捞几个钱来渡过了眼

bought a favourite of Mr. Lin's—a platter of stewed pork. In addition, there was a pint of yellow wine. A smile never left Miss Lin's face, for business in the shop was good, her new silk dress was finished, and because they were fighting back against the Japanese in Shanghai. Mrs. Lin's hiccups were especially sparse— about one every ten minutes.

Only Mr. Lin was sunk in gloom. Moodily drinking his wine, he looked at his daughter, and looked at his wife. Several times he considered dropping the bad news in their midst like a bombshell, but he didn't have that kind of courage. Moreover, he still hadn't given up hope, he still wanted to struggle; at least he wanted to conceal his failure to make ends meet.

And so when the Merchants Guild passed a resolution to pay the soldiers five thousand dollars and asked Mr. Lin to contribute twenty, he consented without a moment's hesitation. He decided not to tell his wife and daughter the true state of affairs until the last possible minute. The way he calculated it was this: He would collect eight per cent of the debts due him, he would pay eighty per cent of the money he owed. Anyhow, he had the excuse that there was fighting in Shanghai, that remittances couldn't be sent. The difficulty was that there was a difference of about six hundred dollars between what people owed him and what he had to pay to others. He would have to take drastic measures and cut prices heavily. The idea was to

59

前再说。这年头儿,谁能够顾到将来呢?眼前得过且过。

是这么想定了方法,又加上那一斤黄酒的力量,林先生倒酣睡了一夜,恶梦也没有半个。

第二天早上,林先生醒来时已经是六点半钟,天色很阴沉。林先生觉得有点头晕。他匆匆忙忙吞进两碗稀饭,就到铺子里,一眼就看见那位上海客人板起了脸孔在那里坐守"回话"。而尤其叫林先生猛吃一惊的,是斜对门的裕昌祥也贴起红红绿绿的纸条,也在那里"大放盘照码九折"了!林先生昨夜想好的"如意算盘"立刻被斜对门那些红绿纸条冲一个摇摇不定。

"林老板,你真是开玩笑!昨晚上不给我回音。轮船是八点钟开,我还得转乘火车,八点钟这班船我是非走不行!请你快点——"

上海客人不耐烦地说,把一个拳头在桌子上一放。林先生只有陪不是,请他原谅,实在是因为上海打仗钱庄不通,彼

scrape together some money to meet the present problem, then he would see. Who could think of the future in times like these? If he could get by now, that would be enough.

That was how he made his plans. With the added potency of the pint of yellow wine, Mr. Lin slept soundly all night, without even the suggestion of a bad dream.

It was already six thirty when Mr. Lin awoke the next morning. The sky was overcast and he was rather dizzy. He gulped down two bowls of rice gruel and hurried to the shop. The first thing to greet his eye was the Shanghai collector, sitting with a stern face, waiting for his "answer." But what shocked Mr. Lin particularly was the shop across the street. They too had pasted red and green strips all over their windows; they too were having a "Big Sale 10% Discount"! Mr. Lin's perfect plan of the night before was completely snowed under by those red and green streamers of his competitor.

"What kind of a joke this, Mr. Lin? Last night you didn't give a reply. That boat leaves here at eight o'clock and I have to make connections with the train. I simply must catch that eight o'clock boat! Please hurry—" said the Shanghai collector impatiently. He brought his clenched fist down on the table

Mr. Lin apologized and begged his forgiveness. Truly, it was all because of the fighting in Shanghai and not being able to send remittances. After all, they

林家铺子

此是多年的老主顾,务请格外看承。

"那么叫我空手回去么?"

"这,这,断乎不会。我们的寿生一回来,有多少付多少,我要是藏落半个钱,不是人!"

林先生颤着声音说,努力忍住了滚到眼眶边的眼泪。

话是说到尽头了,上海客人只好不再噜苏,可是他坐在那里不肯走。林先生急得什么似的,心是卜卜地乱跳。近年他虽然万分拮据,面子上可还遮得过;现在摆一个人在铺子里坐守,这件事要是传扬开去,他的信用可就完了,他的债户还多着呢,万一群起效尤,他这铺子只好立刻关门。他在没有办法中想办法。几次请这位讨账客人到内宅去坐,然而讨账客人不肯。

天又索索地下起冻雨来了。一条街上冷清清地简直没有人行。自有这条街以来,从没见过这样萧索的腊尾岁尽。朔风吹着那些招牌,嚓嚓地响。渐渐地冻雨又有变成雪花的模样。沿街店铺里的伙计们靠在柜台上仰起了脸发怔。

had been doing business for many years. Mr. Lin pleaded for a little special consideration.

"Then am I to go back empty-handed?"

"Why, why, certainly not. When Shousheng returns, I'll give you as much as he brings. I'm not a man if I keep so much as half a dollar!" Mr. Lin's voice trembled. With an effort he held back the tears that brimmed to his eyes.

There was no more to be said: the Shanghai collector stopped his grumbling. But he remained firmly seated where he was. Mr. Lin was nearly out of his wits with anxiety. His heart thumped erratically. Although he had been having a hard time the past few years, he had been able to keep up a front. Now there was a collector sitting in his shop for all the world to see. If word of this thing spread, Mr. Lin's credit would be ruined. He had plenty of creditors. Suppose they all decided to follow suit? His shop might just as well close down immediately. In desperation, several times he invited the Shanghai gentleman to wait in the back room where it was more comfortable, but the latter refused.

An icy rain began to fall. The street was cold and deserted. Never had it appeared so mournful at New Year's time. Signboards creaked and clattered in the grip of a north wind. The icy rain seemed like to turn into snow. In the shops that lined the street, salesmen leaning on the counters looked up blankly.

林先生和那位收账客人有一句没一句的闲谈着。林小姐忽然走出蝴蝶门来站在街边看那索索的冻雨。从蝴蝶门后送来的林大娘的呃呃的声音又渐渐儿加勤。林先生嘴里应酬着,一边看看女儿,又听听老婆的打呃,心里一阵一阵酸上来,想起他的一生简直毫没幸福,然而又不知道坑害他到这地步的,究竟是谁。那位上海客人似乎气平了一些了,忽然很恳切地说:

"林老板,你是个好人。一点嗜好都没有,做生意很巴结认真。放在二十年前,你怕不发财么?可是现今时势不同,捐税重,开销大,生意又清,混得过也还是你的本事。"

林先生叹一口气苦笑着,算是谦逊。

上海客人顿了一顿,又接着说下去:

"贵镇上的市面今年又比上年差些,是不是?内地全靠乡庄生意,乡下人太穷,真是没有法子,——呀,九点钟了!怎么你们的收账伙计还没来呢?这个人靠得住么?"

Occasionally, Mr. Lin and the collector from Shanghai exchanged a few desultory words. Miss Lin suddenly emerged through the swinging doors and stood at the front window watching the cold hissing rain. From the back room, the sound of Mrs. Lin's hiccups steadily gathered intensity. While trying to be pleasant to their visitor, Mr. Lin looked at his daughter and listened to his wife's hiccups, and a wave of depression rose in his breast. He thought how all his life he had never known any prosperity, nor could he imagine who was responsible for his being reduced to such dire straits today.

The Shanghai collector seemed to have calmed down somewhat. "Mr. Lin," he said abruptly, in a sincere tone, "you're a good man. You don't go in for loose living, you're obliging and honest in your business practices. Twenty years ago, you would have gotten rich. But things are different today. Taxes are high, expenses are heavy, business is slow—it's an accomplishment just to get along."

Mr. Lin sighed and smiled in wry modesty.

After a pause, the Shanghai collector continued, "This year the market in this town was a little worse than last, wasn't it? Places in the interior like this depend on the people from the countryside for business, but the peasants are too poor. There's really no solution.... Oh, it's nine o'clock! Why hasn't your collection clerk come back yet? Is he reliable?"

林先生心里一跳,暂时回答不出来。虽然是七八年的老伙计,一向没有出过岔子,但谁能保到底呢!而况又是过期不见回来。上海客人看着林先生那迟疑的神气,就笑;那笑声有几分异样。忽然那边林小姐转脸对林先生急促地叫道:

"爸爸,寿生回来了!一身泥!"

显然林小姐的叫声也是异样的,林先生跳起来,又惊又喜,着急的想跑到柜台前去看,可是心慌了,两腿发软。这时寿生已经跑了进来,当真是一身泥,气喘喘地坐下了,说不出话来。林先生估量那情形不对,吓得没有主意,也不开口。上海客人在旁边皱眉头。过了一会儿,寿生方才喘着气说:

"好险呀!差一些儿被他们抓住了。"

"到底是强盗抢了快班船么?"

林先生惊极,心一横,倒逼出话来了。

"不是强盗。是兵队拉夫呀!昨天下午赶不上趁快班。今天一早趁航船,哪里知道航船听得这里要提船,就停在东栅外了。我上岸走不到半里

Mr. Lin's heart gave a leap. For the moment, he couldn't answer. Although Shousheng had been his salesman for seven or eight years and had never made a slip, still, there was no absolute guarantee! And besides he was overdue. The Shanghai collector laughed to see Mr. Lin's doubtful expression, but his laugh had an odd ring to it.

At the window, Miss Lin whirled and cried urgently, "Papa, Shou-sheng is back! He's covered with mud!"

Her voice had a peculiar sound too. Mr. Lin jumped up, both alarmed and happy. He wanted to run out and look, but he was so excited that his legs were weak. By then Shousheng had already entered, truly covered with mud. The clerk sat down, panting for breath, unable to say a word. The situation looked bad. Frightened out of his wits, Mr. Lin was speechless too. The Shanghai collector frowned. After a while, Shousheng managed to gasp:

"Very dangerous! They nearly got me!"

"Then the boat was robbed?" the agitated Mr. Lin took a grip on himself and blurted.

"There wasn't any robbing. They were grabbing coolies for the army. I couldn't make the boat yesterday afternoon; I got a sampan this morning. After we sailed, we heard they were waiting at this end to grab the boat, so we came to port further down the river. When we got ashore, before we had come half a *li*, we

路,就碰到拉夫。西面宝祥衣庄的阿毛被他们拉去了。我跑得快,抄小路逃了回来。他妈的,性命交关!"

寿生一面说,一面撩起衣服,从肚兜里掏出一个手巾包来递给了林先生,又说道:

"都在这里了。栗市的那家黄茂记很可恶,这种户头,我们明年要留心!——我去洗一个脸,换件衣服再来。"

林先生接了那手巾包,捏一把;脸上有些笑容了。他到账台里打开那手巾包来。先看一看那张"清单",打了一会儿算盘,然后点检银钱数目:是大洋十一元,小洋二百角,钞票四百二十元,外加即期庄票两张,一张是规元五十两,又一张是规元六十五两。这全部付给上海客人,照账算也还差一百多元。林先生凝神想了半晌,斜眼偷看了坐在那里吸烟的上海客人几次,方才叹一口气,割肉似的拿起那两张庄票和四百元钞票捧到上海客人跟前,又说了许多话,方才得到上海客人

bumped into an army pressgang. They grabbed the clerk from the clothing shop, but I ran fast and came back by a short cut. Damn it! It was a close call!"

Shousheng lifted his jacket as he talked and pulled from his money belt a cloth-bound packet which he handed to Mr. Lin.

"It's all here," he said. "That Huang Shop in Lishi is rotten. We have to be careful of customers like that next year.... I'll come back after I have a wash and change my clothes."

Mr. Lin's face lit up as he squeezed the packet. He carried it over to the cashier's cage and unbound the cloth wrapping. First he added up the money due on the list of debtors, then he counted what had been collected. There were eleven silver dollars, two hundred dimes, four hundred and twenty dollars in banknotes, and two bank demand drafts—for the equivalent of fifty and sixty-five taels of silver respectively, at the official rate. If he turned the whole lot over to the Shanghai collector, it would still be more than a hundred dollars short of what he owed the wholesale house.

Deep in contemplation, Mr. Lin glanced several times out of the corner of his eye at the Shanghai collector who was silently smoking a cigarette. At last he sighed, and as though cutting off a piece of his living flesh, placed the two bank drafts and four hundred dollars in cash before the man from Shanghai. Then Mr. Lin spoke for a long time until he managed to extract a

点一下头,说一声"对啦"。

但是上海客人把庄票看了两遍,忽又笑着说道:

"对不起,林老板,这庄票,费神兑了钞票给我罢!"

"可以,可以。"

林先生连忙回答,慌忙在庄票后面盖了本店的书柬图章,派一个伙计到恒源庄去取现,并且叮嘱了要钞票。又过了半晌,伙计却是空手回来。恒源庄把票子收了,但不肯付钱;据说是扣抵了林先生的欠款。天是在当真下雪了,林先生也没张伞,冒雪到恒源庄去亲自交涉,结果是徒然。

"林老板,怎样了呢?"

看见林先生苦着脸跑回来,那上海客人不耐烦地问了。

林先生几乎想哭出来,没有话回答,只是叹气。除了央求那上海客人再通融,还有什么别的办法?寿生也来了,帮着林先生说。他们赌咒:下欠的二百多元,赶明年初十边一定汇到上海。是老主顾了,向来三节清账,从没半句话,今儿实在是意外之变,大局如此,没有办法,非是他们刁赖。

nod from the latter and the words "all right."

But when the collector looked twice at the bank drafts, he said with a smile, "Sorry to trouble you, Mr. Lin. Please get them cashed for me first."

"Certainly, certainly," Mr. Lin hastened to reply. He quickly affixed his shop's seal to the back of the drafts and dispatched one of his salesmen to cash them at the local bank. In a little while, the salesman came back empty-handed. The bank had accepted the drafts but refused to pay for them, saying they would be credited against Mr. Lin's debt. Though it was snowing heavily now, Mr. Lin rushed over to the bank without an umbrella to plead in person. But his efforts were in vain.

"Well, what about it?" demanded the Shanghai collector impatiently as Mr. Lin returned to the shop, his face anguished.

Mr. Lin seemed ready to weep. There was nothing he could say; he could only sigh. Except to beg the collector for more leniency, what else could he do? Shousheng came out and added his pleas to Mr. Lin's. He vowed that they would send the remaining two hundred dollars to Shanghai by the tenth of the new year. Mr. Lin was an old customer who had always paid his debts promptly without a word, said Shousheng. This thing today was really unexpected. But that was the situation; they couldn't help themselves. It wasn't that they were stalling.

然而不添一些,到底是不行的。林先生忍痛又把这几天内卖得的现款凑成了五十元,算是总共付了四百五十元,这才把那位叫人头痛的上海收账客人送走了。

此时已有十一点了,天还是飘飘扬扬落着雪。买客没有半个。林先生纳闷了一会儿,和寿生商量本街的账头怎样去收讨。两个人的眉头都皱紧了,都觉得本镇的六百多元账头收起来真没有把握。寿生挨着林先生的耳朵悄悄地说道:

"听说南栅的聚隆,西栅的和源,都不稳呢!这两处欠我们的,就有三百光景,这两笔倒账要预先防着,吃下了,可不是玩的!"

林先生脸色变了,嘴唇有点抖。不料寿生把声音再放低些,支支吾吾地说出了更骇人的消息来:

"还有,还有讨厌的谣言,是说我们这里了。恒源庄上一定听得了这些风声,这才对我们逼得那么急,说不定上海的收账客人也有点晓得——只是,谁和我们作对呢?难道就是斜对门么?"

寿生说着,就把嘴向裕昌

The Shanghai collector was adamant. Painfully, Mr. Lin brought out the fifty dollars he had taken in during the past few days and handed it over to make up a total payment of four hundred and fifty dollars. Only then did that headache of a Shanghai collector depart.

By that time, it was eleven in the morning. Snowflakes were still drifting down from the sky. Not even half a customer was in sight. Mr. Lin brooded a while, then discussed with Shousheng means to be used in collecting outstanding bills in town. Both men were frowning; neither of them had any particular confidence that much of the six hundred dollars due from town customers could be collected. Shousheng bent close to Mr. Lin's ear and whispered:

"I hear that the big shop at the south gate and the one at the west gate are both shaky. Both of them owe us money—about three hundred dollars altogether. We better take precautions with these two accounts. If they fold up before we can collect, it won't be so funny!"

Mr. Lin paled; his lips trembled a little. Then, Shousheng pitched his voice lower still, and mumbled a bit of even more shocking news.

"There's another nasty rumour—about us. They're sure to have heard it at the bank. That's why they're pressing us so hard. The Shanghai collector probably got wind of it too. Who can be trying to make trouble for us? The shop across the street?"

Shousheng pointed with his pursed lips in the di-

祥那边呶了一呶。林先生的眼光跟着寿生的嘴也向那边瞥了一下,心里直是乱跳,哭丧着脸,好半天说不出话来。他的又麻又痛的心里感到这一次他准是毁了!——不毁才是作怪:党老爷敲诈他,钱庄压逼他,同业又中伤他,而又要吃倒账,凭谁也受不了这样重重的磨折罢?而究竟为了什么他应该活受罪呀!他,从父亲手里继承下这小小的铺子,从没敢浪费;他,做生意多么巴结;他,没有害过人,没有起过歹心;就是他的祖上,也没害过人,做过歹事呀!然而他直如此命苦!

"不过,师傅,随他们去造谣罢,你不要发急。荒年传乱话,听说是镇上的店铺十家有九家没法过年关。时势不好,市面清得不成话,素来硬朗的铺子今年都打饥荒,也不是我们一家困难!天塌压大家,商会里总得议个办法出来;总不能大家一齐拖倒,弄得市面更加不像市面。"

看见林先生急苦了,寿生姑且安慰着,忍不住也叹了一口气。

rection of the suspect, and Mr. Lin's eyes swung to follow the indicator. His heart skipping unevenly, his face mournful, Mr. Lin was unable to speak for some time. He had the numb and aching feeling that this time he was definitely finished! If he weren't ruined it would be a miracle: The Kuomintang chieftains were putting the squeeze on him; the bank was pressing him; his fellow shopkeepers were stabbing him in the back; a couple of his biggest debtors were going to default. Nobody could stand up under this kind of buffeting. But why was he fated to get such a dirty deal? Ever since he inherited the little shop from his father, he had never dared to be wasteful. He had been so obliging; he never hurt a soul, never schemed against anyone. His father and grandfather had been the same, yet all he was reaping was bitterness!

"Never mind. Let them spread their rumours. You don't have to worry," Shousheng tried to comfort Mr. Lin, though he couldn't help sighing himself. "There are always rumours in lean years. They say in this town nine out of ten shops won't be able to pay up their debts before the year is out. Times are bad, the market is dead as a doornail. Usually strong shops are hard up this year. We're not the only one having rough going! When the sky tumbles everyone gets crushed. The Merchants Guild has to think of a way out. All the shops can't be collapsing; that would make the market even less like a market."

雪是愈下愈密了,街上已经见白。偶尔有一条狗垂着尾巴走过,抖一抖身体,摇落了厚积在毛上的那些雪,就又悄悄地夹着尾巴走了。自从有这条街以来,从没见过这样冷落凄凉的年关!而此时,远在上海,日本军的重炮正在发狂地轰毁那边繁盛的市廛。

五

凄凉的年关,终于也过去了。镇上的大小铺子倒闭了二十八家。内中有一家"信用素著"的绸庄。欠了林先生三百元货账的聚隆与和源也毕竟倒了。大年夜的白天,寿生到那两个铺子里磨了半天,也只拿了二十多块来;这以后,就听说没有一个收账员拿到半文钱,两家铺子的老板都躲得不见面了。林先生自己呢,多亏商会长一力斡旋,还无须往乡下躲,然而欠下恒源钱庄的四百多元非要正月十五以前还清不可;并且又订了苛刻的条件:从正月初五开市那天起,恒源就要派人到林先生铺子里"守提",

The snowfall was becoming heavier; it was sticking to the ground now. Occasionally, a dog would slink by, shivering, its tail between its legs. It might stop and shake itself violently to dislodge the snow thickly matting its fur. Then, with tail drooping again, the dog would go on its way. Never in its history had this street witnessed so frigid and desolate a New Year season! And just at this time, in distant Shanghai, Japanese heavy artillery was savagely pounding that prosperous metropolis of trade.

V

It was a gloomy New Year, but finally it was passed. In town, twenty-eight big and little shops folded up, including a "credit A-I" silk shop. The two stores that owed Mr. Lin three hundred dollars closed down too. The last day of the year, Shousheng had gone to them and plagued them for hours, but all he could extract was a total of twenty dollars. He heard that afterwards no other collector got so much as a penny out of them; the owners of the two shops hid themselves and couldn't be found. Thanks to the intervention of the head of the Merchants Guild, it wasn't necessary for Mr. Lin to hide. But he had to guarantee to wipe off his debt of four hundred dollars to the bank before the fifteenth of the first month, and he had to consent to very harsh terms: The bank would send a representative to "guard" all cash taken in starting from

卖得的钱,八成归恒源扣账。

新年那四天,林先生家里就像一个冰窖。林先生常常叹气,林大娘的打呃像连珠炮。林小姐虽然不打呃,也不叹气,但是呆呆地好像害了多年的黄病。她那件大绸新旗袍,为的要付吴妈的工钱,已经上了当铺;小学徒从清早七点钟就去那家唯一的当铺门前守候,直到九点钟方才从人堆里拿了两块钱挤出来。以后,当铺就止当了。两块钱!这已是最高价。随你值多少钱的贵重衣饰,也只能当得两块呢!叫做"两块钱封门"。乡下人忍着冷剥下身上的棉袄递上柜台去,那当铺里的伙计拿起来抖了一抖,就直丢出去,怒声喊道:"不当!"

元旦起,是大好的晴天。关帝庙前那空场上,照例来了跑江湖赶新年生意的摊贩和变把戏的杂耍。人们在那些摊子面前懒懒地拖着腿走,两手扪着空的腰包,就又懒懒地走开了。孩子们拉住了娘的衣角,

resumption of business on the fifth; eighty per cent of all money collected would go to the bank until Mr. Lin's debt to them was paid.

During the New Year holidays, Mr. Lin's house was like an ice box. Mr. Lin heaved sigh after sigh. Mrs. Lin's hiccups were like a string of firecrackers. Miss Lin, although she neither hiccuped nor sighed, moped around in the dazed condition of one who has suffered from years of jaundice. Her new silk dress had already gone to the only pawnshop in town to raise money for the maid's wages. An apprentice had taken it there at seven in the morning; it was after nine when he finally squeezed his way out of the crowd with two dollars in his hand. Afterwards, the pawnshop refused to do any more business that day. Two dollars! That was the highest price they would give for any article, no matter how much you had paid for it originally! This was called "two dollar ceiling." When a peasant, steeling himself against the cold, would peel off a cotton-padded jacket and hand it across the counter, the pawnshop clerk would raise it up, give it a shake, then fling it back with an angry "We don't want it!"

Since New Year's Day, the weather had been beautiful and clear. The big temple courtyard, as was the custom, was crowded with the stalls of itinerant pedlars and the paraphernalia of acrobats and jugglers. People lingered before the stalls, patted their empty money belts, and reluctantly walked on. Children

赖在花炮摊前不肯走,娘就给他一个老大的耳光。那些特来赶新年的摊贩们连伙食都开销不了,白赖在"安商客寓"里,天天和客寓主人吵闹。

只有那班变把戏的出了八块钱的大生意,党老爷们唤他们去点缀了一番"升平气象"。

初四那天晚上,林先生勉强筹措了三块钱,办一席酒请铺子里的"相好"吃照例的"五路酒",商量明天开市的办法。林先生早就筹思过熟透:这铺子开下去呢,眼见得是亏本的生意,不开呢,他一家三口儿简直没有生计,而且到底人家欠他的货账还有四五百,他一关门更难讨取;惟一的办法是减省开支,但捐税派饷是逃不了的,"敲诈"尤其无法躲避,裁去一两个店员罢,本来他只有三个伙计,寿生是左右手,其余的两位也是怪可怜见的,况且辞歇了到底也不够招呼生意;家里呢,也无可再省,吴妈早已辞

dragged at their mothers' clothing, refusing to leave the stall where fireworks were on sale, until Mama was forced to give the little offender a hard slap. The pedlars, who had come specially to cash in on the usual New Year's bazaar trade, didn't even make enough to pay for their food. They couldn't pay their rent at the local inn and quarrelled with the innkeeper every day.

Only the acrobatic troupe earned the large sum of eight dollars. It had been hired by the Kuomintang chieftains to add to the atmosphere of "peace and normalcy."

On the evening of the fourth, Mr. Lin, who had with some difficulty managed to raise three dollars, gave the usual spread for his employees at which they all discussed the strategy for the morrow's re-opening of business. The prospects were already terribly clear to Mr. Lin: If they re-opened, they were sure to operate at a loss; if they didn't re-open, he and his family would be entirely without resources. Moreover, people still owed him four hundred dollars, the collection of which would be even more difficult, if he closed down. The only way out was to cut expenses. But taxes and levies for the soldiers were inescapable; there was even less chance of his avoiding being "squeezed." Fire a couple of salesmen? He only had three. Shousheng was his righthand man; the other two were poor devils; besides he really needed them to wait on the customers. He couldn't save any more at home. They had already

歇。他觉得只有硬着头皮做下去，或者靠菩萨的保佑，乡下人春蚕熟；他的亏空还可以补救。

但要开市，最大的困难是缺乏货品。没有现钱寄到上海去，就拿不到货。上海打得更厉害了，赊账是休转这念头。卖底货罢，他店里早已淘空，架子上那些装卫生衣的纸盒就是空的，不过摆在那里装幌子。他铺子里就剩了些日用杂货，脸盆毛巾之类，存底还厚。

大家喝了一会闷酒，抓腮挖耳地想不出好主意。后来谈起闲天来，一个伙计忽然说。

"乱世年头，人比不上狗！听说上海闸北烧得精光，几十万人都只逃得一个光身子。虹口一带呢，烧是还没烧，人都逃光了，东洋人凶得很，不许搬东西。上海房钱涨起几倍。逃出来的人都到乡下来了，昨天镇上就到了一批，看样子都是好

let the maid go. He felt the only thing to do was to plunge on. Perhaps, when the peasants, with Buddha's blessing, earned money from their spring raw silk sales, he still might make up his loss.

But the greatest problem in resuming business was that he was short of merchandise. Without money to remit to Shanghai, he couldn't replenish his stock. The fighting in Shanghai was getting worse. There was no use in hoping for getting anything on credit. Sell his reserve? The shop was long since actually cleaned out. The underwear boxes on the shelves were empty; they were used only for show. All that was left were things like wash-basins and towels. But he had plenty of those.

Gloomily, the feasters sipped their wine. For all their perplexed reflection, no one could offer any solution to the problem. They talked of generalities for a while. Then suddenly Ah si, one of the salesmen, said:

"The world is going to hell. People live worse than dogs! They say Zhabei was completely burned out. A couple of hundred thousand people had to flee, leaving all their belongings behind. There wasn't any fire in the Hongkou section, but everybody ran away. The Japanese are very cruel. They wouldn't let them take any of their things with them. House rent in safe quarters in Shanghai has skyrocketed. All the refugees are running to the countryside. A bunch came to our

好的人家,现在却弄得无家可归!"

林先生摇头叹气。寿生听了这话,猛的想起了一个好办法;他放下了筷子,拿起酒杯来一口喝干了,笑嘻嘻对林先生说道:

"师傅,听得阿四的话么?我们那些脸盆,毛巾,肥皂,袜子,牙粉,牙刷,就可以如数销清了。"

林先生瞪出了眼睛,不懂得寿生的意思。

"师傅,这是天大的机会。上海逃来的人,总还有几个钱,他们总要买些日用的东西,是不是?这笔生意,我们赶快张罗。"

寿生接着又说,再筛出一杯酒来喝了,满脸是喜气。两个伙计也省悟过来了,哈哈大笑。只有林先生还不很了然。近来的逆境已经把他变成糊涂。他惘然问道:

"你拿得稳么?脸盆,毛巾,别家也有,——"

"师傅,你忘记了!脸盆毛巾一类的东西只有我们存底独多!裕昌祥里拿不出十只脸盆,而且都是拣剩货。这笔生意,逃不出我们的手掌心的了!

town yesterday. They all look like decent people, and now they're homeless!"

Mr. Lin shook his head and sighed, but Shousheng, on hearing these words, was suddenly struck with a bright idea. He put down his chopsticks, then raised his wine cup and drained it in one swallow. He turned to Mr. Lin with a grin.

"Did you hear what Ah si just said? That means our washbasins, wash-cloths, soap, socks, tooth powder, tooth brushes, will sell fast. We can get rid of as many as we've got."

Mr. Lin stared. He didn't know what Shousheng was driving at.

"Look, this is a heaven-sent chance. The Shanghai refugees should have a little money, and they need the usual daily necessities, don't they? We ought to set up right away to handle this business!"

Shousheng poured himself another cup of wine, and drank, his face beaming. The two salesmen caught on, and they began to laugh. Only Mr. Lin was not entirely clear. He had been rather dulled by his recent adversity.

"Are you sure?" he asked, irresolutely. "Other shops have wash-cloths and wash-basins too—"

"But we're the only ones with any real reserve of that sort of stuff. They don't have even ten wash-basins across the street, and those are all seconds. We've got this piece of business right in the palm of our hand!

我们赶快多写几张广告到四栅去分贴,逃难人住的地方——嗳,阿四,他们住在什么地方?我们也要去贴广告。"

"他们有亲戚的住到亲戚家里去了,没有的,还借住在西栅外茧厂的空房子。"

叫做阿四的伙计回答,脸上发亮,很得意自己的无意中立了大功。林先生这时也完全明白了。心里一快乐,就又灵活起来,他马上拟好了广告的底稿,专拣店里有的日用品开列上去,约莫也有十几种。他又摹仿上海大商店卖"一元货"的方法,把脸盆,毛巾,牙刷,牙粉配成一套卖一块钱,广告上就大书"大廉价一元货"。店里本来还有余剩下的红绿纸,寿生大张的裁好了,拿笔就写。两个伙计和学徒就乱烘烘地拿过脸盆,毛巾,牙刷,牙粉来装配成一组。人手不够,林先生叫女儿出来帮着写,帮着扎配,另外又配出几种"一元货",全是零星的日用必需品。

Let's write a lot of ads and paste them up at the town's four gateways, any place in town where the refugees are staying—say, Ashi, where *are* they living? We'll go put up our stickers there!"

"The ones with relatives here are living with their relatives. The rest have borrowed that empty building in the silk factory outside the west gate." Ah si's face shone with satisfaction over the excellent result he had unwittingly produced.

At last, Mr. Lin had the whole picture. Happy, his spirits revived. He immediately drafted the wording of the advertisements, listing all the daily necessities which the shop had available for sale. There were over a dozen different commodities. In imitation of the big Shanghai stores, he adopted the "One Dollar Package" technique. For a dollar the customer would get a wash-basin, a wash-cloth, a tooth brush and a box of tooth powder. "Big Dollar Sale!" screamed the ad in huge letters. Shousheng brought out the shop's remaining sheets of red and green paper and cut them into large strips. Then he took up his brush and started writing. The salesmen and the apprentices noisily collected the wash-basins, wash-cloths, tooth brushes and boxes of tooth powder, and arranged them into sets. There weren't enough hands for all the work. Mr. Lin called his daughter out to help with writing the ads and tying the packages. He also made up other kinds of combination packages—all of daily necessities.

这一晚上,林家铺子里直忙到五更左右,方才大致就绪。第二天清早,开门鞭炮响过,排门开了,林家铺子布置得又是一新。漏夜赶起来的广告早已漏夜分头贴出去。西栅外茧厂一带是寿生亲自去布置,哄动那些借住在茧厂里的逃难人,都起来看,当做一件新闻。

"内宅"里,林大娘也起了个五更,瓷观音面前点了香,林大娘爬着磕了半天响头。她什么都祷告全了,就只差没有祷告菩萨要上海的战事再扩大再延长,好多来些逃难人。

一切都很顺利,一切都不出寿生的预料。新正开市第一天就只林家铺子生意很好,到下午四点多钟,居然卖了一百多元,是这镇上近十年来未有的新纪录。销售的大宗,果然是"一元货",然而洋伞橡皮雨鞋之类却也带起了销路,并且那生意也做的干脆有味。虽然是"逃难人",却毕竟住在上海,见过大场面,他们不像乡下人

That night, they were busy in the shop late and long. At dawn they had things pretty much in order. When the popping of firecrackers heralded the opening of business the next morning, the shop of the Lin family again had a new look. Their advertisements had already been pasted up all over town. Shousheng had personally attended to the silk factory outside the west gate. The ad with which he plastered the factory walls struck the eyes of the refugees, and they all crowded around to read it as if it were a news bulletin.

In the "inner sanctum" Mrs. Lin, too, rose very early. She lit incense before the porcelain image of the Goddess Kuanyin and kowtowed for a considerable time, knocking her head resoundingly against the floor. She prayed for practically everything. About the only thing she omitted was a plea for more refugees to come to the town.

It all worked out fine, just as Shousheng had predicted. Mr. Lin's shop was the only one whose trade was brisk on the first business day after the New Year's holidays. By four in the afternoon, he had sold over one hundred dollars' worth of merchandise—the highest figure for a day ever reached in that town in the past ten years. His biggest seller was the "One Dollar Package," and it served as a leader to such items as umbrellas and rubber overshoes. Business, moreover, went smoothly, pleasantly. The refugees came from Shanghai, after all; they were used to the ways of the

或本镇人那么小格式,他们买东西很爽利,拿起货来看了一眼,现钱交易,从不拣来拣去,也不硬要除零头。

林大娘看见女儿兴冲冲地跑进来夸说一回,就爬到瓷观音面前磕了一回头。她心里还转了这样的念头:要不是岁数相差得多,把寿生招做女婿倒也是好的!说不定在寿生那边也时常用半只眼睛看望着这位厮熟的十七岁的"师妹"。

只有一点,使林先生扫兴;恒源庄毫不顾面子地派人来提取了当天营业总数的八成。并且存户朱三阿太,桥头陈老七,还有张寡妇,不知听了谁的怂恿,都借了"要量米吃"的借口,都来预支息金;不但支息金,还想拔提一点存款呢!但也有一个喜讯,听说又到了一批逃难人。

晚餐时,林先生添了两碟荤菜,酬劳他的店员。大家称赞寿生能干。林先生虽然高

big city; they weren't as petty as the townspeople or peasants from the out-lying districts. When they bought something, they made up their minds quickly. They'd pick up a thing, look at it, then produce their money. There was none of this pawing through all the merchandise, no haggling over a few pennies.

When her daughter, all flushed and excited, rushed into the back room for a moment to report the good business, Mrs. Lin went to kowtow before the porcelain Kuanyin again. If Shou-sheng weren't twice the gril's age, Mrs. Lin was thinking, wouldn't he make a good son-in-law! And it wasn't at all unlikely that Shousheng had half an eye on his employer's seventeen-year-old daughter, this girl whom he knew so well.

There was just one thing that spoiled Mr. Lin's happiness—completely disregarding his dignity, the local bank had sent its man to collect eighty per cent of the sales proceeds. And he didn't know who egged them on, but the three creditors of the shop, on the excuse that they "needed a little money to buy rice," all showed up to draw out some advance interest. Not only interest; they even wanted repayment of part of their loans too! But Mr. Lin also heard some good news—another batch of refugees had arrived in town.

For dinner that evening, Mr. Lin served two additional meat dishes, by way of reward to his employees. Everyone complimented Shousheng on his shrewdness.

兴,却不能不惦念着朱三阿太等三位存户要提存款的事情。大新年碰到这种事,总是不吉利。寿生愤然说:

"那三个懂得什么呢!还不是有人从中挑拨!"

说着,寿生的嘴又向斜对门呶了一呶。林先生点头。可是这三位不懂什么的,倒也难以对付;一个是老头子,两个是孤苦的女人,软说不肯,硬来又不成。林先生想了半天觉得只有去找商会长,请他去和那三位宝贝讲开。他和寿生说了,寿生也竭力赞成。

于是晚饭后算过了当天的"流水账",林先生就去拜访商会长。

林先生说明了来意后,那商会长一口就应承了,还夸奖林先生做生意的手段高明,他那铺子一定能够站住,而且上进。摸着自己的下巴,商会长又笑了一笑,伛过身体来说道:

"有一件事,早就想对你说,只是没有机会。镇上的卜局长不知在哪里见过令爱来,

Although Mr. Lin was happy, he couldn't help thinking of how his three creditors had talked about being repaid their loans. It was unlucky to have such a thing happen at the beginning of the new year.

"What do they know!" said Shousheng angrily. "Somebody must have put them up to it!" He pointed with his lips at the shop across the street.

Mr. Lin nodded. But whether the three creditors knew anything or not, it was going to be difficult to handle them. An old man and two widows. You couldn't be soft with them, but getting tough wouldn't either. Mr. Lin pondered for some time, and finally decided the best thing to do would be to ask the head of the Merchants Guild to speak to his three precious creditors. He asked Shousheng for his opinion. Shousheng heartily agreed.

When dinner was over, and Mr. Lin had added up his receipts for the day, he went to pay his respects to the head of the Merchants Guild. The latter expressed complete approval of Mr. Lin's idea. What's more, he commended Mr. Lin on the intelligent way in which he conducted his business. He said the shop was sure to stand firm, in fact it would improve. Stroking his chin, the head of the Merchants Guild smiled and leaned towards Mr. Lin.

"There's something I've been wanting to talk to you about for a long time, but I never had the opportunity. I don't know where Kuomintang Commissioner Pu

极为中意;卜局长年将四十,还没有儿子,屋子里虽则放着两个人,都没生育过;要是令爱过去,生下一男半女,就是现成的局长太太。呵,那时,就连我也沾点儿光呢!"

林先生做梦也想不到会有这样的难题,当下怔住了做不得声。商会长却又郑重地接着说:

"我们是老朋友。什么话都可以讲个明白。论到这种事呢,照老派说,好像面子上不好听;然而也不尽然。现在通行这一套,令爱过去也算是正的。——况且,卜局长既然有了这个心,不答应他有许多不便之处;答应了,将来倒有巴望。我是替你打算,才说这个话。"

"咳,你怕不是好意劝我仔细!可是,我是小户人家,小女又不懂规矩,高攀卜局长,实在不敢!"

林先生硬着头皮说,心里卜卜乱跳。

saw your daughter, but he's very interested in her. Commissioner Pu is forty and he had no sons. Though he has two women at home, neither of them has been able to give birth. If your daughter should join his household and present him with a child, he's sure to make her his wife, Madam Commissioner. Ah, if that should happen, even I could share in the reflected glory!"

Never in his wildest dreams had Mr. Lin ever imagined he would run into trouble like this. He was speechless. The head of the Merchants Guild continued solemnly:

"We're old friends. There's nothing we can't speak freely about to each other. This kind of thing, according to the old standards, would make you lose face. But it isn't altogether like that any more; it's quite common nowadays. Your daughter's going over could be considered proper marriage. Anyhow, since that is what Commissioner Pu has in mind, there might be some inconvenience if you refuse him. If you agree, you can have real hope for the future. I wouldn't be telling you this if I didn't have your interests at heart."

"Of course in advising me to be careful, your intentions are the best! But I'm an unimportant person, my daughter knows nothing of high society. We don't dare aspire so high as a commissioner!" Mr. Lin had to brace himself up to speak. His heart was thumping fast.

"哈,哈,不是你高攀,是他中意。——就这么罢,你回去和尊夫人商量商量,我这里且搁着,看见卜局长时,就说还没机会提过,行不行呢?可是你得早点给我回音!"

"嗯——"

筹思了半晌,林先生勉强应着,脸色像是死人。

回到家里,林先生支开了女儿,就一五一十对林大娘说了。他还没说完,林大娘的呃就大发作,光景邻舍都听得清。她勉强抑住了那些涌上来的呃,喘着气说道:

"怎么能够答应,呃,就不是小老婆,呃,呃——我也舍不得阿秀到人家去做媳妇。"

"我也是这个意思,不过——"

"呃,我们规规矩矩做生意,呃,难道我们不肯,他好抢了去不成?呃——"

"不过他一定要来找讹头生事!这种人比强盗还狠心!"

林先生低声说,几乎落下眼泪来。

"我拼了这条老命。呃!救苦救难观世音呀!"

林大娘颤着声音站了起来,摇摇摆摆想走。林先生赶快拦住,没口地叫道:

"Ha ha! It isn't a question of your aspirations, but the fact that he finds her suitable.... Let's leave it at that. You go home and talk it over with your wife. I'll put the matter aside. When I see Commissioner Pu I'll say I haven't had a chance to speak to you about it, alright? But you must give me an answer soon!"

There was a long pause. Then, "I will," Mr. Lin forced himself to say. His face was ghastly.

When he got home, he sent his daughter out of the room and reported to his wife in detail. Even before he finished, Mrs. Lin's hiccups rose in a powerful barrage that was probably audible to all the neighbours. With an effort she stemmed the tide and said, panting:

"How can we consent? —hic—Even if it wasn't concubine he wanted hic—hic—even if he were looking for a wife, I still couldn't bear to part with her!"

"That's the way I feel, but—"

"Hic—we run our business all legal and proper. Do you mean to say if we don't agree he could get away with taking her by force? Hic—"

"But he's sure to find an excuse to make some kind of trouble. That kind of man is crueler than a bandit!" Mr. Lin whispered. He was nearly crying.

"He'll get her only over my dead body! Hic! Goddess Kuanyin preserve us!" cried Mrs. Lin in a voice that trembled. She rose and started to sway out of the room. Mr. Lin hastily barred her way.

"往哪里去？往哪里去？"

同时林小姐也从房外来了，显然已经听见了一些，脸色灰白，眼睛死瞪瞪地。林大娘看见女儿，就一把抱住了，一边哭，一边打呃，一边喃喃地挣扎着喘着气说：

"呃，阿囡，呃，谁来抢你去，呃，我同他拼老命！呃，生你那年我得了这个——病，呃，好容易养到十七岁，呃，呃，死也死在一块儿！呃，早给了寿生多么好呢！呃！强盗！不怕天打的！"

林小姐也哭了，叫着"妈！"林先生搓着手叹气。看看哭得不像样，窄房浅屋的要惊动邻舍，大新年也不吉利，他只好忍着一肚子气来劝母女两个。

这一夜，林家三口儿都没有好生睡觉。明天一早林先生还得起来做生意，在一夜的转侧愁思中，他偶尔听得屋面上一声响，心就卜卜地跳，以为是

"Where are you going? Where are you going?" he babbled.

Just then, Miss Lin came in. Obviously she had overheard quite a bit, for her complexion was the colour of chalk and her eyes were staring fixedly. Mrs. Lin flung her arms around her daughter and wept and hiccuped while she struggled to say in gasps:

"Hic—child—hic—anybody who tries to snatch you—hic—will have to do it over my dead body! Hic! The year I gave birth to you I got this—sickness—hic— It was hard, but I brought you up till now you're seventeen—hic—hic—Dead or alive, we'll stick together! Hic! We should have promised you to Shousheng long ago! Hic! That Pu is a dirty crook! He isn't afraid the gods will strike him down!"

Miss Lin wept too, crying "Ma!" Mr. Lin wrung his hands and sighed. The women were wailing at an alarming rate, and he was afraid their laments would be heard through the thin walls and startle the neighbours. This sort of row was also an unlucky way to commence the new year. Holding his own emotions in check, he did his best to soothe wife and daughter.

That night, all three members of the Lin family slept badly. Although Mr. Lin had to get up early the next morning to go to business, he wrestled with his gloomy thoughts all night. A sudden sound on the roof sent his heart leaping with fear that Commissioner Pu

卜局长来寻他生事来了；然而定了神仔细想起来，自家是规规矩矩的生意人，又没犯法，只要生意好，不欠人家的钱，难道好无端生事，白诈他不成？而他的生意呢，眼前分明有一线生机。生了个女儿长的还端正，却又要招祸！早些定了亲，也许不会出这岔子？——商会长是不是肯真心帮忙呢，只有恳求他设法——可是林大娘又在打呃了，咳，她这病！

天刚发白，林先生就起身，眼圈儿有点红肿，头里发昏。可是他不能不打起精神招呼生意。铺面上靠寿生一个到底不行，这小伙子近几天来也就累得够了。

林先生坐在账台里，心总不定。生意虽然好，他却时时浑身的肉发抖。看见面生的大汉子上来买东西，他就疑惑是卜局长派来的人，来侦察他，来寻事；他的心直跳得发痛。

却也作怪，这天生意之好，

had come to trump up charges against him. Then he calmed himself and considered the matter carefully. His was a family of proper business people who had never committed any crimes. As long as he did a good business and didn't owe people money, surely Pu couldn't make trouble without any reason at all. And now Lin's business was beginning to show some vitality. Just because he had raised a good-looking daughter, he had invited disaster! He should have engaged her years ago, then maybe this problem would never have arisen.... Was the head of the Merchants Guild sincerely willing to help? The only way out was to beg for his aid—Mrs. Lin started hiccuping again. Ai! That ailment of hers!

Mr. Lin rose as soon as the sky began to turn light. His eyes were somewhat bloodshot and swollen, and he felt dizzy. But he had to pull himself together and attend to business. He couldn't leave the entire management of the shop to Shousheng; the young fellow had put in an exhausting few days.

He was still uneasy after he seated himself in the cashier's cage. Although business was good, from time to time his whole body was shaken by violent shivers. Whenever a big man came in, if Mr. Lin didn't know him, he would suspect that the man had been sent by Commissioner Pu to spy, to stir up a fuss, and his heart would thump painfully.

And it was strange. Business that day was active

出人意料。到正午,已经卖了五六十元,买客们中间也有本镇人。那简直不像买东西,简直是抢东西,只有倒闭了铺子拍卖底货的时候才有这种光景。林先生一边有点高兴,一边却也看着心惊,他估量"这样的好生意气色不正"。果然在午饭的时候,寿生就悄悄告诉道:

"外边又有谣言,说是你拆烂污卖一批贱货,捞到几个钱,就打算逃走!"

林先生又气又怕,开不得口。突然来了两个穿制服的人,直闯进来问道:

"谁是林老板?"

林先生慌忙站了起来,还没回答,两个穿制服的拉住他就走。寿生追上去,想要拦阻,又想要探询,那两个人厉声吆喝道:

"你是谁?滚开!党部里要他问话!"

六

那天下午,林先生就没有回来。店里生意忙,寿生又不能抽空身子尽自去探听。里边

beyond all expectations. By noon they had sold nearly sixty dollar's worth of merchandise. There were local townspeople among the customers too. They weren't just buying; they were practically grabbing. The only thing like it would be a bankrupt shop selling its stock out at auction cheap. While Mr. Lin was fairly pleased, he was also rather alarmed. This kind of business didn't look healthy to him. Sure enough, Shousheng approached him during the lunch hour and said softly:

"There's a rumour outside that you've cut prices to clear out your left-overs. That when you've collected a little money, you're going to take it and run!"

Mr. Lin was both angry and frightened. He couldn't speak. Suddenly two men in uniform entered and barged forward to demand:

"Which one is Mr. Lin, the proprietor?"

Mr. Lin rose in flurred haste. Before he had a chance to reply, the uniformed men began to lead him away. Shousheng came over to stop them and to question them. They barked at him savagely:

"Who are you? Stand aside! He's wanted for questioning at the Kuomintang office!"

VI

That afternoon, Mr. Lin did not return. They were busy at the shop, and Shousheng could not get away to inquire personaly. He had managed to conceal

林大娘本来还被瞒着,不防小学徒漏了嘴,林大娘那一急几乎一口气死去。她又死不放林小姐出那对蝴蝶门儿,说是:

"你的爸爸已经被他们捉去了,回头就要来抢你!呃——"

她只叫寿生进来问底细,寿生瞧着情形不便直说,只含糊安慰了几句道:

"师母,不要着急,没有事的!师傅到党部里去理直那些存款呢。我们的生意好,怕什么的!"

背转了林大娘的面,寿生悄悄告诉林小姐,"到底为什么,还没得个准信儿,"他叮嘱林小姐且安心伴着"师母",外边事有他呢。林小姐一点主意也没有,寿生说一句,她就点一下头。

这样又要招顾外面的生意,又要挖空心思找出话来对付林大娘不时的追询,寿生更没有工夫去探听林先生的下落。直到上灯时分,这才由商会长给他一个信:林先生是被党部扣住了,为的外边谣言林先生打算卷款逃走,然而林先生除有庄款和客账未清外,还

the truth from Mrs. Lin but one of the apprentices let it leak out, and the lady became frantic almost to the point of distraction. She absolutely refused to let Miss Lin go out of the swinging doors.

"They've already taken your father. They'll be coming back for you next! Hic—"

She called in Shousheng and questioned him closely. He didn't think it advisable to tell her too much.

"Don't worry, Mrs. Lin," he comforted. "There's nothing wrong! He only went down to the Kuomintang office to straighten out the question of our creditors. Business is good. What have we got to be afraid of!"

Behind Mrs. Lin's back, he told Miss Lin quietly, "We still don't really know what this is all about." He urged her to look after her mother; he would attend to the shop. Miss Lin didn't have the faintest idea what to do. She agreed to everything Shousheng said.

Between waiting on the customers and thinking up answers to Mrs. Lin's constant questions, it was impossible for Shousheng to find time to inquire about the fate of Mr. Lin. Finally, at twilight, word was brought by the head of the Merchants Guild: Mr. Lin was being held by the Kuomintang chieftains because of the rumour that he was planning to abscond with the shop's money. Besides what Mr. Lin owed the bank and the wholesale house, there were also his three poor credi-

有朱三阿太、桥头陈老七、张寡妇三位孤苦人儿的存款共计六百五十元没有保障,党部里是专替这些孤苦人儿谋利益的,所以把林先生扣起来,要他理直这些存款。

寿生吓得脸都黄了,呆了半晌,方才问道：

"先把人保出来,行么？人不出来,哪里去弄钱来呢？"

"嘿！保出人来！你空手去,让你保么？"

"会长先生,总求你想想法子,做好事。师傅和你老人家向来交情也不差,总求你做做好事！"

商会长皱着眉头沉吟了一会儿,又端相着寿生半晌,然后一把拉寿生到屋角里悄悄说道：

"你师傅的事,我岂有袖手旁观之理。只是这件事现在弄僵了！老实对你说,我求过卜局长出面讲情,卜局长只要你师傅答应一件事,他是肯帮忙的;我刚才到党部里会见你的师傅,劝他答应,他也答应了,那不是事情完了么？不料党部里那个黑麻子真可恶,他硬不

106

tors to be considered. The total of six hundred and fifty dollars which they had put up was in jeopardy. The Kuomintang was especially concerned over the welfare of these poor people. So it was detaining him until he settled with them.

Shousheng's face was drained of colour. Dazed, he finally managed to ask:

"Can we put up a guarantee and have him released first? Unless we get him out, how are we going to raise the money?"

"Huh! Release him on a guarantee! You can't become his guarantor if you go there without money in your hands!"

"Mr. Guild Leader, think of something, I beg you. Do a good deed. You and Mr. Lin are old friends. I beg you to help him!"

The head of the Merchants Guild frowned thoughtfully. He looked at Shousheng for a minute, then led him to a corner of the room and said in a low voice:

"I can't stand by with folded arms and watch Mr. Lin remain in difficulty. But the situation is very strained now! To tell you the truth, I've already pleaded with Commissioner Pu to intervene. Commissioner Pu only wanted Mr. Lin to agree to one thing, and would be willing to help him. I've just seen Mr. Lin at the Kuomintang office where I urged him to consent, and he did so. Shouldn't that be the end of the matter? Who would have thought that dark pock-marked fellow

肯——"

"难道他不给卜局长面子？"

"就是呀！黑麻子反而噜哩噜苏说了许多，卜局长几乎下不得台。两个人闹翻了！这不是这件事弄得僵透？"

寿生叹了口气，没有主意；停一会儿，他又叹一口气说：

"可是师傅并没犯什么罪。"

"他们不同你讲理！谁有势，谁就有理！你去对林大娘说，放心，还没吃苦，不过要想出来，总得花点儿钱！"

商会长说着，伸两个指头一扬，就匆匆地走了。

寿生沉吟着，没有主意；两个伙计攒住他探问，他也不回答。商会长这番话，可以告诉"师母"么？又得花钱！"师母"有没有私蓄，他不知道；至于店里，他很明白，两天来卖得的现钱，被恒源提了八成去，剩下只有五十多块，济得什么事！商会长示意总得两百。知道还够

in the Kuomintang would be so nasty? He still insists—"

"Surely he wouldn't go against Commissioner Pu?"

"That's what I thought! But the pock-marked fellow kept mumbling and grumbling till Commissioner Pu was very embarrassed. They had a terrible row! Now you see how awkward things are?"

Shousheng sighed. He had no idea. There was a pause, then he sighed again and said:

"But Mr. Lin hasn't committed any crime."

"Those people don't talk reason! With them, might makes right! Tell Mrs. Lin not to worry; Mr. Lin hasn't been mistreated yet. But to get him out she'll have to spend a little money!"

The head of the Merchants Guild held up two fingers, then quickly departed.

Though he racked his brains, Shousheng could see no other alternative. The two salesmen palgued him with questions, but he ignored them. He was wondering whether he should report the words of the head of the Merchants Guild to Mrs. Lin. Again they had to spend money! While he didn't know quite clear as to the financial condition of the shop: After the local bank got through deducting its eighty per cent from the cash earned during the past two days, all that was left for the shop was about fifty dollars. A lot of good that would do! The head of the Merchants Guild had indi-

不够呀!照这样下去,生意再好些也不中用。他觉得有点灰心了。

里边又在叫他了!他只好进去瞧光景再定主意。

林大娘扶住了女儿的肩头,气喘喘地问道:

"呃,刚才,呃——商会长来了,呃,说什么?"

"没有来呀!"

寿生撒一个谎。

"你不用瞒我,呃——我,呃,全知道了;啊,你的脸色吓得焦黄!阿秀看见的,呃!"

"师母放心,商会长说过不要紧。——卜局长肯帮忙——"

"什么?呃,呃——什么?卜局长肯帮忙!——呃,呃,大慈大悲的菩萨,呃,不要他帮忙!呃,呃,我知道,你的师傅,呃呃,没有命了!呃,我也不要活了!呃,只是这阿秀,呃,我放心不下!呃,呃,你同了她去!呃,你们好好的做人家!呃,呃,寿生,呃,你待阿秀好,我就放心了!呃,去呀!他们要来抢!呃——狠心的强盗!

cated a bribe of two hundred dollars. Who knew whether that would be enough! The way things were, even if business should improve even more, it still wouldn't be any use. Shousheng felt discouraged.

From the back room, someone was calling him. He decided to go in and size up the situation, and then determined what should be done. He found Mrs. Lin leaning on her daughter's arm.

"Hic—just now —hic —the head of the Merchants Guild came — hic —" she panted. "What did he say?"

"He wasn't here," lied Shousheng.

"You can't fool me — hic — I — hic — know everything. Hic — your face is scared yellow! Xiu saw him—hic!"

"Be calm, Mrs. Lin. He says it's all right. Commissioner Pu is willing to help—"

"What? Hic — hic — What? Commissioner Pu is willing to help! —hic, hic — Merciful goddess — hic — I don't want his help! Hic, hic — I know Mr. Lin — hic, hic — is finished! Hic — I want to die too! There's only Xiu — hic — that I'm worried about! Hic, hic — take her with you! — hic! You two go and get married! Hic — hic — Shousheng — hic — you take good care of Xiu and I won't worry about anything! Hic! Go! They want to grab her! —

111

观世音菩萨怎么不显灵呀！"

寿生睁大了眼睛，不知道怎样回话。他以为"师母"疯了，但可又一点不像疯。他偷眼看他的"师妹"，心里有点跳；林小姐满脸通红，低了头不作声。

"寿生哥，寿生哥，有人找你说话！"

小学徒一路跳着喊进来。寿生慌忙跑出去，总以为又是商会长什么的来了，哪里知道竟是斜对门裕昌祥的掌柜吴先生。"他来干什么？"寿生肚子里想，眼光盯住在吴先生的脸上。

吴先生问过了林先生的消息，就满脸笑容，连说"不要紧"。寿生觉得那笑脸有点异样。

"我是来找你划一点货——"

吴先生收了笑容，忽然转了口气，从袖子里摸出一张纸来。是一张横单，写着十几行，正是林先生所卖"一元货"的全部。寿生一眼瞧见就明白了，原来是这个把戏呀！他立刻说：

"师傅不在，我不能作主。"

"你和你师母说，还不是一样！"

112

hic — the savage beasts! Goddess Kuanyin, why don't you display your divine power!"

Shousheng stared. He didn't know what to say. He thought Mrs. Lin had gone mad, yet she didn't look the least abnormal. His heart beating hard, he stole a glance at Miss Lin. She was blushing scarlet; she kept her head down and made no comment.

"Shousheng, Shousheng, somebody wants to see you!" an apprentice came running in and announced.

Thinking it was the head of the Merchants Guild or some such personage, Shousheng rushed out. To his surprise, he found Mr. Wu, proprietor of the shop across the street, waiting for him. What does he want? wondered Shousheng. He fixed his eyes on Mr. Wu's face.

Mr. Wu inquired about Mr. Lin, and then, all smiles, said he was sure it was "not serious." Shousheng felt there was something fishy about his smile.

"I've come to buy a little of your merchandise—" The smile had disappeared from Mr. Wu's face and the tone of his voice changed. He produced a sheet of paper from his sleeve. It was a list of over a dozen items—the very things Mr. Lin was featuring in his "One Dollar Package." One look and Shousheng understood. So that was the game!

"Mr. Lin isn't here," he said promptly. "I haven't the right to decide."

"Why not talk to Mrs. Lin? That'll be just as

寿生踌躇着不能回答。他现在有点懂得林先生之所以被捕了。先是谣言林先生要想逃，其次是林先生被扣住了，而现在却是裕昌祥来挖货，这一连串的线索都明白了。寿生想来有点气，又有点怕，他很知道，要是答应了吴先生的要求，那么，林先生的生意，自己的一番心血，都完了。可是不答应呢，还有什么把戏来，他简直不敢想下去了。最后他姑且试一试说：

"那么，我去和师母说，可是，师母女人家专要做现钱交易。"

"现钱么？哈，寿生，你是说笑话罢？"

"师母是这种脾气，我也是没法。最好等明天再谈罢。刚才商会长说，卜局长肯帮忙讲情，光景师傅今晚上就可以回来了。"

寿生故意冷冷的说，就把那张横单塞还吴先生的手里。吴先生脸上的肉一跳，慌忙把横单又推回到寿生手里，一面没口应承道：

"好，好，现账就是现账。今晚上交货，就是现账。"

good!"

Shousheng hesitated to reply. He was beginning to have an inkling of why Mr. Lin had been detained. First there was the rumour that Mr. Lin was planning to run away, then Mr. Lin was arrested, and now the competitor's shop had come to gouge merchandise. There was an obvious connection between these events. Shousheng became rather angry, and a bit frightened. He knew that if he agreed to Mr. Wu's request, Mr. Lin's business would be finished, and the heart's blood that he himself had expended would be in vain. But if he refused, what other tricks would be forthcoming? He simply didn't dare to think.

"I'll go and talk to Mrs. Lin, then," he offered tentatively. "But she only operates on a cash basis."

"Cash? Ha, Shousheng, of course you're joking?"

"That's the kind of person Mrs. Lin is. I can't do anything with her. The best thing would be for you to come again tomorrow. The head of the Merchants Guild just told me that Commissioner Pu is willing to take a hand in the matter. Mr. Lin probably will be back tonight," said Shousheng with cold deliberateness. He shoved the list back in Mr. Wu's hand.

His face twitching, the latter hastily forced the list on Shousheng again.

"All right, all right, if it has to be cash then it's cash. I'll take the goods tonight. Cash on delivery."

寿生皱着眉头再到里边,把裕昌祥来挖货的事情对林大娘说了,并且劝她:

"师母,刚才商会长来,确实说师傅好好的在那里,并没吃苦;不过总得花几个钱,才能出来。店里只有五十块。现在裕昌祥来挖货,照这单子上看,总也有一百五十块光景,还是挖给他们罢,早点救师傅出来要紧!"

林大娘听说又要花钱,眼泪直淌,那一阵呃,当真打得震天响,她只是摇手,说不出话,头靠在桌子上,把桌子捣得怪响。寿生瞧来不是路,悄悄的退出去,但在蝴蝶门边,林小姐追上来了。她的脸色像死人一样白,她的声音抖而且哑,她急口地说:

"妈是气糊涂了!总说爸爸已经被他们弄死了!你,你赶快答应裕昌祥,赶快救爸爸!寿生哥,你——"

林小姐说到这里,忽然脸一红,就飞快地跑进去了。寿生望着她的后影,呆立了半分

Scowling, Shousheng walked into the back room and told Mrs. Lin about the shop across the street wanting to gouge merchandise.

"When the head of the Merchants Guild was here, he really said Mr. Lin was fine; he hasn't been through any hardships. But we'll have to spend some money to get him out. There's only fifty dollars in the shop. Now this fellow across the street wants goods—from the looks of his list, about a hundred and fifty dollars' worth. Why not let him have them? The important thing is to get Mr. Lin back as soon as possible!"

Upon hearing that they had to spend money again, tears gushed from Mrs. Lin's eyes, and her hiccups truly shook the heavens with their intensity. Beyond words, she could only wave her hand, while her head, which she rested on the table, resounded alarmingly against the wooden top. Shousheng could see that he was getting nowhere, and he quietly withdrew. Miss Lin caught up with him outside the swinging doors. Her face was deathly white, her voice trembling and hoarse.

"Ma is so angry she can't think straight," Miss Lin whispered urgently. "She keeps saying they're already killed Papa! You, you hurry up and agree to what Mr. Wu wants. Save Papa, quick! Shousheng, Brother, you—" At this point, her face suddenly flamed scarlet, and she flew back into the room.

In a daze, Shousheng stared after her for a full

钟光景,然后转身,下决心担负这挖货给裕昌祥的责任,至少"师妹"是和他一条心要这么办了。

夜饭已经摆在店铺里了,寿生也没有心思吃,立等着裕昌祥交过钱来,他拿一百在手里,另外身边藏了八十,就飞跑去找商会长。

半点钟后,寿生和林先生一同回来了。跑进"内宅"的时候,林大娘看见了倒吓一跳。认明是当真活的林先生时,林大娘急急爬在瓷观音前磕响头,比她打呃的声音还要响。林小姐光着眼睛站在旁边,像是要哭,又像是要笑。寿生从身旁掏出一个纸包来,放在桌子上说:

"这是多下来的八十块钱。"

林先生叹了一口气,过一会儿,方才有声没气地说道:

"让我死在那边就是了,又花钱弄出来!没有钱,大家还是死路一条!"

林大娘突然从地下跳起来,着急的想说话,可是一连串的呃把她的话塞住了。林小姐

half minute, then he turned away, determined to take the responsibility for selling the merchandise to their competitor. At least Miss Lin agreed with him on what should be done.

The table had already been laid for dinner in the shop, but Shousheng had no appetite. As soon as Mr. Wu arrived with the money, Shousheng took one hundred dollars in his hand and concealed another eighty dollars on his person, and rushed off to find the head of the Merchants Guild.

Half an hour later Shou-shneg returned with Mr. Lin. Bursting into the "inner sanctum," they nearly startled Mrs. Lin out of her wits. When she saw that it was really Mr. Lin in the flesh, she agitatedly prostrated herself before the porcelain Kuanyin and kowtowed vigorously, pounding her head so loudly that it drowned out the sound of her hiccups. Miss Lin stood to one side, her eyes staring. She looked as if she wanted to laugh and cry at the same time. Shousheng took out a paper-wrapped packet and set it on the table.

"This is eighty dollars we didn't have to use."

Mr. Lin sighed. When he finally spoke, his voice was dull.

"You should have let me die there and be done with it. Spending more money to get me out! Now we've got no money, we're all going to die anyhow!"

Mrs. Lin jumped up from the ground, excited and wanting to speak. But a string of hiccups blocked the

忍住了声音,抽抽咽咽地哭。林先生却还不哭,又叹一口气,梗咽着说:

"货是挖空了!店开不成,债又逼的紧——"

"师傅!"

寿生叫了一声,用手指蘸着茶,在桌子上写了一个"走"字给林先生看。

林先生摇头,眼泪扑簌簌地直淌;他看看林大娘,又看看林小姐,又叹一口气。

"师傅!只有这一条路了。店里并凑起来,还有一百块,你带了去,过一两个月也就够了;这里的事,我和他们理直。"

寿生低声说。可是林大娘却偏偏听得了,她忽然抑住了呃,抢着叫道:

"你们也去!你,阿秀。放我一个人在这里好了,我拼老命!呃!"

忽然异常少健起来,林大娘转身跑到楼上去了。林小姐叫着"妈",随后也追了上去。林先生望着楼梯发怔,心里感到有什么要紧的事,却又乱麻麻地总是想不起。寿生又低声

words in her throat. Miss Lin wept quietly, with suppressed sobs. Mr. Lin did not cry. He sighed again and said in a choked voice:

"Our merchandise has been cleaned out! We can't do any business, they're pressing us hard for debts—"

"Mr. Lin!"

It was Shousheng who shouted. He dipped his finger in the tea, then wrote on the table the one word—"Go."

Mr. Lin shook his head. Tears flowed from his eyes. He looked at his wife, he looked at his daughter, and again he sighed.

"That's the only way out, Mr. Lin! We can still scrape together a hundred dollars in the shop. Take it with you; it'll be enough for a month or two. I'll take care of what has to be done here."

Although Shousheng spoke quietly, Mrs. Lin overheard him. She curbed her hiccups and interjected:

"You go too, Shousheng! You and Xiu. Leave me here alone. I'll fight to the death! Hic!"

Mrs. Lin suddenly appeared remarkably young and healthy; she whirled and ran up the stairs. "Ma!" called Miss Lin, and dashed after her mother. Mr. Lin stared at the stairway, bewildered. He felt he had something important to say, but he was too numb to recall what it was.

说：

"师傅，你和师妹一同走罢！师妹在这里，师母是不放心的！她总说他们要来抢——"

林先生淌着眼泪点头，可是打不起主意。

寿生忍不住眼圈儿也红了，叹一口气，绕着桌子走。

忽然听得林小姐的哭声。林先生和寿生都一跳。他们赶到楼梯头时，林大娘却正从房里出来，手里捧一个皮纸包儿。看见林先生和寿生都已在楼梯头了，她就缩回房去，嘴里说"你们也来，听我的主意"。她当着林先生和寿生的跟前，指着那纸包说道：

"这是我的私房，呃，光景有两百多块。分一半你们拿去。呃！阿秀，我做主配给寿生！呃，明天阿秀和她爸爸同走。呃，我不走！寿生陪我几天再说。呃，知道我还有几天活，呃，你们就在我面前拜一拜，我也放心！呃——"

林大娘一手拉着林小姐，一手拉着寿生，就要他们"拜一拜"。

都拜了，两个人脸上飞红，都低着头。寿生偷眼看林小姐，看见她的泪痕中含着一些笑意，寿生心头卜卜地跳了，反

"You and Xiu go together," Shousheng urged softly. "Mrs. Lin will worry if Xiu stays here! She says they want to snatch—"

Tears in his eyes, Mr. Lin nodded. He couldn't make up his mind.

Shousheng felt his own eyes smarting. He sighed and walked around the table.

Just then, they heard Miss Lin crying. Startled, Mr. Lin and Shousheng rushed up the stairs. Mrs. Lin was coming out of her room with a paper packet in her hand. She went back into the room when she saw them, and said:

"Please come in, both of you. Listen to what I've decided." She pointed at the packet. "In here is my private property—hic—about two hundred dollars. I'm giving you two half. Hic! Xiu, I give you in marriage to Shousheng! Hic—tomorrow, Xiu and her father will leave together. Hic—I'm not going! Shousheng will stay with me a few days, and then we'll see. Who knows how many days I have left to live—hic— So if you both kowtow in my presence, I can set my mind at ease! Hic—"

Mrs. Lin took her daughter by one hand and Shousheng by the other, and ordered them to "kowtow." Both did so, their cheeks flaming red; they kept their heads down. Shousheng stole a glance at Miss Lin. There was a faint smile on her tear-stained face.

123

倒落下两滴眼泪。

林先生松一口气,说道;

"好罢,就是这样。可是寿生,你留在这里对付他们,万事要细心!"

七

林家铺子终于倒闭了。林老板逃走的新闻传遍了全镇。债权人中间的恒源庄首先派人到林家铺子里封存底货。他们又搜寻账簿。一本也没有了。问寿生。寿生躺在床上害病。又去逼问林大娘。林大娘的回答是连珠炮似的打呃和眼泪鼻涕。为的她到底是"林大娘",人们也没有办法。

十一点钟光景,大群的债权人在林家铺子里吵闹得异常厉害。恒源庄和其他的债权人争执怎样分配底货。铺子里虽然淘空,但连"生财"合计,也足够偿还债权者七成,然而谁都只想给自己争得九成或竟至十成。商会长说得舌头都有点僵硬了,却没有结果。

来了两个警察,拿着木棍

His heart thumped wildly, and two tears rolled down from his eyes.

"Good. That's the way it'll be." Mr. Lin heaved a sigh. "But Shousheng, when you stay here and deal with those people, be very, very careful!"

VII

The shop of the Lin family had to close down at last. The news that Mr. Lin had run away soon spread all over town. Of the creditors, the local bank was the first to send people to put the stock into custody. They also searched for the account books. Not one was to be found. They asked for Shousheng. He was sick in bed . They grilled Mrs. Lin. Her reply was a string of explosive hiccups and a stream of tears. Since she after all enjoyed the social position of "Madam Lin," there was nothing they could do with her.

By about eleven a.m., the horde of creditors in the Lin shop were quarrelling with a tremendous din. The local bank and the other creditors were wrangling as to how to divide the remaining property. Although the stock was nearly gone, the remainder and the furniture and fixture were enough to repay the creditors about seventy per cent; but each was fighting for a ninety, or even one hundred, per cent for himself. The head of the Merchants Guild had talked until his tongue was a little paralysed, to no avail.

Two policemen arrived and took their stand out-

站在门口吆喝那些看热闹的闲人。

"怎么不让我进去?我有三百块钱的存款呀!我的老本!"

朱三阿太扭着瘪嘴唇和警察争论,巍颤颤地在人堆里挤。她额上的青筋就有小指头儿那么粗。她挤了一会儿,忽然看见张寡妇抱着五岁的孩子在那里哀求另一个警察放她进去。那警察斜着眼睛,假装是调弄那孩子,却偷偷地用手背在张寡妇的乳部揉摸。

"张家嫂呀——"

朱三阿太气喘喘地叫了一声,就坐在石阶沿上,用力地扭着她的瘪嘴唇。

张寡妇转过身来,找寻是谁唤她;那警察却用了亵昵的口吻叫道:

"不要性急!再过一会儿就进去!"

听得这句话的闲人都笑起来了。张寡妇装作不懂,含着一泡眼泪,无目的地又走了一步。恰好看见朱三阿太坐在石阶沿上喘气。张寡妇跌撞似的也到了朱三阿太的旁边,也坐在那石阶沿上,忽然就放声大哭。她一边哭,一边喃喃地诉说着:

"阿大的爷呀,你丢下我去了,你知道我是多么苦啊!强盗兵打杀了你,前天是三周年……绝子绝孙的林老板又倒了铺子,——我十个指头做出来

side the shop door. Clubs in hand, they barked at the crowed that had gathered to see the excitement.

"Why can't I go in? I've got a three hundred dollar loan in this shop! My savings!" Mrs. Zhu argued with a policeman, twisting her withered lips. Tottering, she was elbowing her way through the mass. The blue veins on her forehead stood out as thick as little fingers. She kept pushing. Then suddenly she saw Widow Zhang, with her five-year-old baby in her arms, pleading with the other policeman to let her enter. He looked at the widow out of the corners of his eyes, and while feigning to tease the child, furtively rubbed the back of his hand against the widow's breasts.

"Sister Zhang—" Mrs. Zhu gasped loudly. She sat down on the edge of the stone steps, forcibly moving her puckered mouth.

Tears in her eyes, Widow Zhang took an aimless step, which brought into her line of vision Mrs. Zhu panting on the edge of the stone stairs. She practically stumbled over to Mrs. Zhu and sat down beside her. Then, Widow Zhang began to cry and lament:

"Oh, my husband, you've left me alone! You don't know how I'm suffering! The wicked soldiers killed you — it was three years ago the day before yesterday.... That cursed Mr. Lin — may he die without sons or grandsons! —has closed his shop! The hundr-

的百几十块钱,丢在水里了,也没响一声!啊哟!穷人命苦,有钱人心狠——"

看见妈哭,孩子也哭了;张寡妇搂住了孩子,哭的更伤心。

朱三阿太却不哭,弩起了一对发红的已经凹陷的眼睛,发疯似的反复说着一句话:

"穷人是一条命,有钱人也是一条命;少了我的钱,我拼老命!"

此时有一个人从铺子里挤出来,正是桥头陈老七。他满脸紫青,一边挤,一边回过头去嚷骂道:

"你们这伙强盗!看你们有好报!天火烧,地火爆,总有一天现在我陈老七眼睛里呀!要吃倒账,就大家吃,分摊到一个边皮儿,也是公平,——"

陈老七正骂得起劲,一眼看见了朱三阿太和张寡妇,就叫着她们的名字说:

"三阿太,张家嫂,你们怎么坐在这里哭!货色,他们分完了!我一张嘴吵不过他们十几张嘴,这班狗强盗不讲理,硬说我们的钱不算账,——"

ed and fifty dollars that I earned by the toil of my two hands has fallen into the sea and is gone without a sound! Aiya! The lot of the poor is hard, and the rich have no hearts—"

Hearing his mother cry, the child also began to wail. Widow Zhang hugged him to her bosom and wept even more bitterly.

Mrs. Zhu did not cry. Her sunken red-rimmed eyes glared, and she kept saying frantically:

"The poor have only one life, and the rich have only one life. If they don't give me back my money, I'll fight them to the death!"

Just then, a man pushed his way out of the shop. It was Old Chen. His face was purple. He was cursing as he jostled through the crowd.

"You gang of crooks! You'll pay for this! One day I'll see you all burning in the fires of Hell! If we have to take a loss, everybody should take it together. Even if I got only a small share of what's left, at least that would be fair—"

Still swearing vigorously, he spotted the two women.

"Mrs. Zhang, Mrs. Zhu, what are you sitting there crying for!" he shouted to them. "They've finished dividing up the property. My one mouth couldn't out-argue their dozen. That pack of jackals doesn't give a damn about what's reasonable. They insist that our money doesn't count—"

张寡妇听说,哭得更加苦了。先前那个警察忽然又踅过来,用木棍子拨着张寡妇的肩膀说:

"喂,哭什么?你的养家人早就死了。现在还哭哪一个!"

"狗屁!人家抢了我们的,你这东西也要来调戏女人么?"

陈老七怒冲冲地叫起来,用力将那警察推了一把。那警察睁圆了怪眼睛,扬起棍子就想要打。闲人们都大喊,骂那警察。另一个警察赶快跑来,拉开了陈老七说:

"你在这里吵,也是白吵。我们和你无怨无仇,商会里叫来守门,吃这碗饭,没办法。"

"陈老七,你到党部里去告状罢!"

人堆里有一个声音这么喊。听声音就知道是本街有名的闲汉陆和尚。

"去,去!看他们怎样说。"

许多声音乱叫了。但是那位作调人的警察却冷笑,扳着陈老七的肩膀道:

"我劝你少找点麻烦罢。到那边,中什么用!你还是等候林老板回来和他算账,他倒不好白赖。"

陈老七虎起了脸孔,弄得没有主意了。经不住那些闲人

His words made Widow Zhang weep more bitterly than ever. The playful policeman abruptly walked over to her. He poked her shoulder with his club.

"Hey, what are you crying about? Your man died a long time ago. Which one are you crying for now!"

"Dog farts!" roared Old Chen furiously. "While those people are stealing our money, all a turd like you can do is get gay with women!" He gave the policeman a strong push.

The policeman's nasty eyes went wide. He raised his club to strike, but the crowd yelled and cursed at him. The other policeman ran over and pulled Old Chen to one side.

"It's no use your raising a fuss. We've got nothing against you. The Merchants Guild has ordered us to guard the door. We've got to eat. We can't help it."

"Old Chen, go make a complaint at the Kuomintang office!" a man shouted from the crowd. From the sound of it, it was the voice of Lu, the well-known loafer.

"Go on, go on!" yelled several others. "See what they say to that!"

The policeman who had mediated laughed coldly. He grasped Old Chen by the shoulder. "I advise you not to go looking for trouble. Going there won't do you any good! You wait till Mr. Lin comes back and settle things with him. He can't deny the debt."

Old Chen fumed. He couldn't make up his mind.

们都撺怂着"去",他就看着朱三阿太和张寡妇说道:

"去去怎样?那边是天天大叫保护穷人的呀!"

"不错。昨天他们扣住了林老板,也是说防他逃走,穷人的钱没有着落!"

又一个主张去的拉长了声音叫。于是不由自主似的,陈老七他们三个和一群闲人都向党部所在那条路去了。张寡妇一路上还是啼哭,咒骂打杀了她丈夫的强盗兵,咒骂绝子绝孙的林老板,又咒骂那个恶狗似的警察。

快到了目的地时,望见那门前排立着四个警察,都拿着棍子,远远地就吆喝道:

"滚开!不准过来!"

"我们是来告状的,林家铺子倒了,我们存在那里的钱都拿不到——"

陈老七走在最前排,也高声的说。可是从警察背后突然跳出一个黑麻子来,怒声喝打。警察们却还站着,只用嘴威吓。陈老七背后的闲人们大噪起来。黑麻子怒叫道:

"不识好歹的贱狗!我们

The idlers were still shouting for him to "go." He looked at Mrs. Zhu and Widow Zhang.

"What do you say? They're always screaming down there how they protect the poor!"

"That's right," called one of the crowd. "Yesterday they arrested Mr. Lin because they said they didn't want him to run away with poor people's money!"

Almost involuntarily, Old Chen and the two women were swept along by the crowed down the street to the Kuomintang office. Widow Zhang was crying as she walked, and cursing the wicked soldiers who had killed her husband, and praying that Mr. Lin should die without sons or grandsons, and reviling that dirty dog of a policeman!

As they neared the office, they saw four policemen standing outside the gate with clubs in their hands. The policemen yelled to them from a distance:

"Go home! You can't go in!"

"We've come to make a complaint!" shouted Old Chen, who was in the first rank of the crowd. "The shop of the Lin family has closed down, and we can't get hold of the money we put to—"

A swarthy pock-marked man jumped out from behind the policemen and howled for them to attack. But the policemen stood their ground, restricting themselves to threats. The crowd in back of Old Chen began to clamour.

"You cheap mongrels don't know what's good for

133

这里管你们那些事么？再不走，就开枪了！"

他跺着脚喝那四个警察动手打。陈老七是站在最前，已经挨了几棍子。闲人们大乱。朱三阿太老迈，跌倒了。张寡妇慌忙中落掉了鞋子，给人们一冲，也跌在地下，她连滚带爬躲过了许多跳过的和踏上来的脚，站起来跑了一段路，方才觉到她的孩子没有了。看衣襟上时，有几滴血。

"啊哟！我的宝贝！我的心肝！强盗杀人了，玉皇大帝救命呀！"

她带哭带嚷的快跑，头发纷散；待到她跑过那倒闭了的林家铺面时，她已经完全疯了！

1932年6月18日作完

you!" screamed the pock-marked man. "Do you think we have nothing better to do than bother about your business? If you don't get out of here, we're going to fire!"

He stamped and yelled at the policemen to use their clubs. In the front ranks, Old Chen was struck several times. The crowd milled in confusion. Mrs. Zhu was old and weak, and she toppled to the ground. In her panicky haste, Widow Zhang lost her slippers. Pushed and buffeted, she also fell down. Rolling and crawling, she avoided many leaping and stamping feet. She scrambled up and ran for all she was worth. It was then she realized that her child was gone. There were drops of blood on the upper part of her jacket.

"Aiya! My precious! My heart! The bandits are killing people! Jade Emperor God save us!"

Wailing, her hair tumbled in disorder, she ran quickly. By the time she fled past the closed door of the shop of the Lin family, she was completely out of her mind.

June 18, 1932

一

老通宝坐在"塘路"边的一块石头上,长旱烟管斜摆在他身边。"清明"节后的太阳已经很有力量,老通宝背脊上热烘烘地,像背着一盆火。"塘路"上拉纤的快班船上的绍兴人只穿了一件蓝布单衫,敞开了大襟,弯着身子拉,额角上黄豆大的汗粒落到地下。

看着人家那样辛苦的劳动,老通宝觉得身上更加热了;热的有点儿发痒。他还穿着那件过冬的破棉袄,他的夹袄还在当铺里,却不防才得"清明"边,天就那么热。

"真是天也变了!"

老通宝心里说,就吐一口浓厚的唾沫。在他面前那条"官河"内,水是绿油油的,来往的船也不多,镜子一样的水面这里那里起了几道皱纹或是小小的涡旋,那时候,倒影在水里的泥岸和岸边成排的桑树,都搅乱成灰暗的一片。可是不会很长久的。渐渐儿那些树影又在水面上显现,一弯一曲地蠕

I

Old Tong Bao sat on a rock beside the road that skirted the canal, his long-stemmed pipe lying on the ground next to him. Though it was only a few days after "Clear and Bright Festival" the April sun was already very strong. It scorched Old Tong Bao's spine like a basin of fire. Straining down the road, the men towing the fast junk wore only thin tunics, open in front. They were bent far forward, pulling, pulling, pulling, great beads of sweat dripping from their brows.

The sight of others toiling strenuously made Old Tong Bao feel even warmer; he began to itch. He was still wearing the tattered padded jacket in which he had passed the winter. His unlined jacket had not yet been redeemed from the pawn shop. Who would have believed it could get so hot right after "Clear and Bright?"

Even the weather's not what it used to be, Old Tong Bao said to himself, and spat emphatically.

Before him, the water of the canal was green and shiny. Occasional passing boats broke the mirror-smooth surface into ripples and eddies, turning the reflection of the earthen bank and the long line of mulberry trees flanking it into a dancing grey blur. But not for long! Gradually the trees reappeared, twisting and

动,像是醉汉,再过一会儿,终于站定了,依然是很清晰的倒影。那拳头模样的桠枝顶都已经簇生着小手指儿那么大的嫩绿叶。这密密层层的桑树,沿着那"官河"一直望去,好像没有尽头。田里现在还只有干裂的泥块,这一带,现在是桑树的势力!在老通宝背后,也是大片的桑林,矮矮的,静穆的,在热烘烘的太阳光下,似乎那"桑拳"上的嫩绿叶过一秒钟就会大一些。

离老通宝坐处不远,一所灰白色的楼房蹲在"塘路"边,那是茧厂。十多天前驻扎过军队,现在那边田里留着几条短短的战壕。那时都说东洋兵要打进来,镇上有钱人都逃光了;现在兵队又开走了,那座茧厂依旧空关在那里,等候春茧上市的时候再热闹一番。老通宝也听得镇上小陈老爷的儿子——陈大少爷说过,今年上海不太平,丝厂都关门,恐怕这里的茧厂也不能开;但老通宝是

weaving drunkenly. Another few minutes, and they were again standing still, reflected as clearly as before. On the gnarled fists of the mulberry branches, little fingers of tender green buds were already bursting forth. Crowded close together, the trees along the canal seemed to march endlessly into the distance. The unplanted fields as yet were only cracked colds of dry earth; the mulberry trees reigned supreme here this time of the year! Behind Old Tong Bao's back was another great stretch of mulberry trees, squat, silent. The little buds seemed to be growing bigger every second in the hot sunlight.

Not far from where Old Tong Bao was sitting, a grey twostorey building crouched beside the road. That was the silk filature, where the delicate fibres were removed from the cocoons. Two weeks ago it was occupied by troops; a few short trenches still scarred the fields around it. Everyone had said that the Japanese soldiers were attacking in this direction. The rich people in the market town had all run away. Now the troops were gone and the silk filature stood empty and locked as before. There would be no noise and excitement in it again until cocoon selling time.

Old Tong Bao had heard Young Master Chen—son of the Master Chen who lived in town—say that Shanghai was seething with unrest, that all the silk weaving factories had closed their doors, that the silk filatures here probably wouldn't open either. But he couldn't

不肯相信的。他活了六十岁，反乱年头也经过好几个，从没见过绿油油的桑叶白养在树上等到成了"枯叶"去喂羊吃；除非是"蚕花"不熟，但那是老天爷的"权柄"，谁又能够未卜先知？

"才得清明边，天就那么热！"

老通宝看着那些桑拳上怒茁的小绿叶儿，心里又这么想，同时有几分惊异，有几分快活。他记得自己还是二十多岁少壮的时候，有一年也是"清明"边就得穿夹，后来就是"蚕花二十四分"，自己也就在这一年成了家。那时，他家正在"发"；他的父亲像一头老牛似的，什么都懂得，什么都做得；便是他那创家立业的祖父，虽说在长毛窝里吃过苦头，却也愈老愈硬朗。那时候，老陈老爷去世不久，小陈老爷还没抽上鸦片烟，"陈老爷家"也不是现在那么不像样的。老通宝相信自己一家和"陈老爷家"虽则一边是高门大户，而一边不过

believe it. He had been through many periods of turmoil and strife in his sixty years, yet he had never seen a time when the shiny green mulberry leaves had been allowed to wither on the branches and become fodder for the sheep. Of course if the silkworm eggs shouldn't ripen, that would be different. Such matters were all in the hands of the Old Lord of the Sky. Who could foretell His will?

"Only just after Clear and Bright and so hot already!" marvelled Old Tong Bao, gazing at the small green mulberry leaves. He was happy as well as surprised. He could remember only one year when it was too hot for padded clothes at Clear and Bright. He was in his twenties then, and the silkworm eggs had hatched "two hundred per cent"! That was the year he got married. His family was flourishing in those days. His father was like an experienced plough ox—there was nothing he didn't understand, nothing he wasn't willing to try. Even his old grandfather—the one who had first started the family on the road to prosperity—seemed to be growing more hearty with age, in spite of the hard time he was said to have had during the years he was a prisoner of the "Long Hairs."

Old Master Chen was still alive then. His son, the present Master Chen, hadn't begun smoking opium yet, and the "House of Chen" hadn't become the bad lot it was today. Moreover, even though the House of Chen was of the rich gentry and his own family only or-

是种田人,然而两家的命运好像是一条线儿牵着。不但"长毛造反"那时候,老通宝的祖父和陈老爷同被长毛掳去,同在长毛窝里混上了六七年,不但他们俩同时从长毛营盘里逃了出来,而且偷得了长毛的许多金元宝——人家到现在还是这么说;并且老陈老爷做丝生意"发"起来的时候,老通宝家养蚕也是年年都好,十年中间挣得了二十亩的稻田和十多亩的桑地,还有三开间两进的一座平屋。这时候,老通宝家在东村庄上被人人所妒羡,也正像"陈老爷家"在镇上是数一数二的大户人家。可是以后,两家都不行了;老通宝现在已经没有自己的田地,反欠出三百多块钱的债,"陈老爷家"也早已完结。人家都说"长毛鬼"在阴间告了一状,阎罗王追还"陈老爷家"的金元宝横财,所以败的这么快。这个,老通宝也有几分相信:不是鬼使神差,好端端的小陈老爷怎么会抽上了鸦片烟?

dinary tillers of the land, Old Tong Bao had felt that the destinies of the two families were linked together. Years ago, "Long Hairs" campaigning through the countryside had captured Tong Bao's grandfather and Old Master Chen and kept them working as prisoners for nearly seven years in the same camp. They had escaped together, taking a lot of the "Long Hairs'" gold with them—people still talk about it to this day. What's more, at the same time Old Master Chen's silk trade began to prosper, the cocoon raising of Tong Bao's family grew successful too. Within ten years grandfather had earned enough to buy three acres of rice paddy, two acres of mulberry grove, and build a modest house. Tong Bao's family was the envy of the people of East Village, just as the House of Chen ranked among the first families in the market town.

But afterwards, both families had declined. Today, Old Tong Bao had no land of his own, in fact he was over three hundred silver dollars in debt. The House of Chen was finished too. People said the spirit of the dead "Long Hairs" had sued the Chens in the underworld, and because the King of Hell had decreed that the Chens repay the fortune they had amassed on the stolen gold, the family had gone down financially very quickly. Old Tong Bao was rather inclined to believe this. If it hadn't been for the influence of devils, why would a decent fellow like Master Chen have taken to smoking opium?

可是老通宝死也想不明白为什么"陈老爷家"的"败"会牵动到他家。他确实知道自己家并没得过长毛的横财。虽则听死了的老头子说,好像那老祖父逃出长毛营盘的时候,不巧撞着了一个巡路的小长毛,当时没法,只好杀了他,——这是一个"结"！然而从老通宝懂事以来,他们家替这小长毛鬼拜忏念佛烧纸锭,记不清有多少次了。这个小冤魂,理应早投凡胎。老通宝虽然不很记得祖父是怎样"做人",但父亲的勤俭忠厚,他是亲眼看见的；他自己也是规矩人,他的儿子阿四,儿媳四大娘,都是勤俭的。就是小儿子阿多年纪青,有几分"不知苦辣",可是毛头小伙子,大都这么着,算不得"败家相"！

老通宝抬起他那焦黄的皱脸,苦恼地望着他面前的那条河,河里的船,以及两岸的桑地。一切都和他二十多岁时差不了多少,然而"世界"到底变了。他自己家也要常常把杂粮当饭吃一天,而且又欠出了三

What Old Tong Bao could never understand was why the fall of the House of Chen should affect his own family. They certainly hadn't kept any of the "Long Hairs'" gold. True, his father had related that when grandfather was escaping from the "Long Hairs'" camp he had run into a young "Long Hair" on pattol and had to kill him. What else could he have done? It was "fate"! Still from Tong Bao's earliest recollections, his family had prayed and offered sacrifices to appease the soul of the departed young "Long Hair" time and time again. That little wronged spirit should have left the nether world and been reborn long ago by now! Although Old Tong Bao couldn't recall what sort of man his grandfather was, he knew his father had been hardworking and honest—he had seen that with his own eyes. Old Tong Bao himself was a respectable person; both Ah Si, his elder son, and his daughter-in-law were industrious and frugal. Only his younger son, Ah Duo, was inclined to be a little flighty. But youngsters were all like that. There was nothing really bad about the boy....

Old Tong Bao raised his srinkled face, scorched by years of hot sun to the colour of dark parchment. He gazed bitterly at the canal before him, at the boats on its waters, at the mulberry trees along its banks. All were approximately the same as they had been when he was twenty. But the world had changed. His family now often had to make their meals of pumpkin instead

百多块钱的债。

呜！呜,呜,呜,——

汽笛叫声突然从那边远远的河身的弯曲地方传了来。就在那边,蹲着又一个茧厂,远望去隐约可见那整齐的石"帮岸"。一条柴油引擎的小轮船很威严地从那茧厂后驶出来,拖着三条大船,迎面向老通宝来了。满河平静的水立刻激起泼剌剌的波浪,一齐向两旁的泥岸卷过来。一条乡下"赤膊船"赶快拢岸,船上人揪住了泥岸上的树根,船和人都好像在那里打秋千。轧轧轧的轮机声和洋油臭,飞散在这和平的绿的田野。老通宝满脸恨意,看着这小轮船来,看着它过去,直到又转一个弯,呜呜呜地又叫了几声,就看不见。老通宝向来仇恨小轮船这一类洋鬼子的东西！他从没见过洋鬼子,可是他从他的父亲嘴里知道老陈老爷见过洋鬼子:红眉毛,绿眼睛,走路时两条腿是直的。并且老陈老爷也是很恨洋鬼子,常常说"铜钿都被洋鬼子骗去了"。老通宝看见老陈老爷的

of rice. He was over three hundred silver dollars in debt....

Toot! Toot-toot-toot....

Far up the bend in the canal a boat whistle broke the silence. There was a silk filature over there too. He could see vaguely the neat lines of stones embedded as reinforcement in the canal bank. A small oil-burning river boat came puffing up pompously from beyond the silk filature, tugging three larger craft in its wake. Immediately the peaceful water was agitated with waves rolling towards the banks on both sides of the canal. A peasant, poling a tiny boat, hastened to shore and clutched a clump of reeds growing in the shallows. The waves tossed him and his little craft up and down like a see-saw. The peaceful green countryside was filled with the chugging of the boat engine and the stink of its exhaust.

Hatred burned in Old Tong Bao's eyes. He watched the river boat approach, he watched it sail past and glared after it until it went tooting around another bend and disappeared from sight. He had always abominated the foreign devils' contraptions. He himself had never met a foreign devil, but his father had given him a description of one Old Master Chen had seen—red eyebrows, green eyes and a stiff-legged walk! Old Master Chen had hated the foreign devils too. "The foreign devils have swindled our money away," he used to say. Old Tong Bao was only eight or nine the last

149

时候,不过八九岁,——现在他所记得的关于老陈老爷的一切都是听来的,可是他想起了"铜钿都被洋鬼子骗去了"这句话,就仿佛看见了老陈老爷捋着胡子摇头的神气。

洋鬼子怎样就骗了钱去,老通宝不很明白。但他很相信老陈老爷的话一定不错。并且他自己也明明看到自从镇上有了洋纱,洋布,洋油,——这一类洋货,而且河里更有了小火轮船以后,他自己田里生出来的东西就一天一天不值钱,而镇上的东西却一天一天贵起来。他父亲留下来的一份家产就这么变小,变做没有,而且现在负了债。老通宝恨洋鬼子不是没有理由的!他这坚定的主张,在村坊上很有名。五年前,有人告诉他:朝代又改了,新朝代是要"打倒"洋鬼子的。老通宝不相信。为的他上镇去看见那新到的喊着"打倒洋鬼子"的年青人们都穿了洋鬼子衣服。他想来这伙年青人一定私通洋

time he saw Old Master Chen. All he remembered about him now were things he had heard from others. But whenever Old Tong Bao thought of that remark— "The foreign devils have swindled our money away"— he could almost picture Old Master Chen, stroking his beard and wagging his head.

How the foreign devils had accomplished this, Old Tong Bao wasn't too clear. He was sure, however, that Old Master Chen was right. Some things he himself had seen quite plainly. From the time foreign goods—cambric, cloth, oil—appeared in the market town, from the time the foreign river boats increased on the canal, what he produced brought a lower price in the market every day, while what he had to buy became more and more expensive. That was why the property his father left him had shrunk until it finally vanished completely; and now he was in debt. It was not without reason that Old Tong Bao hated the foreign devils!

In the village, his attitude towards foreigners was well known. Five years before, in 1927, someone had told him: The new Kuomintang government says it wants to "throw out" the foreign devils. Old Tong Bao didn't believe it. He heard those young propaganda speech makers the Kuomintang sent when he went into the market town. Though they cried "Throw out the foreign devils," they were dressed in Western style clothing. His guess was that they were secretly in

151

鬼子,却故意来骗乡下人。后来果然就不喊"打倒洋鬼子"了,而且镇上的东西更加一天一天贵起来,派到乡下人身上的捐税也更加多起来。老通宝深信这都是串通了洋鬼子干的。

然而更使老通宝去年几乎气成病的,是茧子也是洋种的卖得好价钱;洋种的茧子,一担要贵上十多块钱。素来和儿媳总还和睦的老通宝,在这件事上可就吵了架。儿媳四大娘去年就要养洋种的蚕。小儿子跟他嫂嫂是一路,那阿四虽然嘴里不多说,心里也是要洋种的。老通宝拗不过他们,末了只好让步。现在他家里有的五张蚕种,就是土种四张,洋种一张。

"世界真是越变越坏!过几年他们连桑叶都要洋种了!我活得厌了!"

老通宝看着那些桑树,心里说,拿起身边的长旱烟管恨恨地敲着脚边的泥块。太阳现在正当他头顶,他的影子落在泥地上,短短地像一段乌焦木头,还穿着破棉袄的他,觉得浑

152

league with the foreign devils, that they had been purposely sent to delude the countryfolk! Sur enough, the Kuomintang dropped the slogan not long after, and prices and taxes rose steadily. Old Tong Bao was firmly convinced that all this occurred as part of a government conspiracy with the foreign devils.

Last year something had happened that made him almost sick with fury: Only the cocoons spun by the foreign strain silkworms could be sold at a decent price. Buyers paid ten dollars more per load for them than they did for the local variety. Usually on good terms with his daughter-in-law, Old Tong Bao had quarrelled with her because of this. She had wanted to raise only foreign silkworms, and Old Tong Bao's younger son Ah Duo had agreed with her. Though Ah Si didn't say much, in his heart he certainly had also favoured this course. Events had proved they were right, and they wouldn't let Old Tong Bao forget it. This year, he had to compromise. Of the five trays they would raise, only four would be silkworms of the local variety; one tray would contain foreign silkworms. "The world's going from bad to worse! In another couple of years they'll even be wanting foreign mulberry trees! It's enough to take all the joy out of life!"

Old Tong Bao picked up his long pipe and rapped it angrily against a cold of dry earth. The sun was directly overhead now, foreshortening his shadow till it looked like a piece of charcoal. Still in his padded

身躁热起来了。他解开了大襟上的钮扣,又抓着衣角扇了几下,站起来回家去。

那一片桑树背后就是稻田。现在大部分是匀整的半翻着的燥裂的泥块。偶尔也有种了杂粮的,那黄金一般的菜花散出强烈的香味。那边远远地一簇房屋,就是老通宝他们住了三代的村坊,现在那些屋上都袅起了白的炊烟。

老通宝从桑林里走出来,到田塍上,转身又望那一片爆着嫩绿的桑树。忽然那边田里跳跃着来了一个十来岁的男孩子,远远地就喊道:

"阿爹!妈等你吃中饭呢!"

"哦——"

老通宝知道是孙子小宝,随口应着,还是望着那一片桑林。才只得"清明"边,桑叶尖儿就抽得那么小指头儿似的,他一生就只见过两次。今年的蚕花,光景是好年成。三张蚕

jacket, he was bathed in heat. He unfastened the jacket and swung its opened edges back and forth a few times to fan himself. Then he stood up and started for home.

Behind the row of mulberry trees were paddy fields. Most of them were as yet only neatly ploughed furrows of upturned earth clods, dried and cracked by the hot sun. Here and there, the early crops were coming up. In one field, the golden blossoms of rape-seed plants emitted a heady fragrance. And that group of houses way over there, that was the village where three generations of Old Tong Bao's family were living. Above the houses, white smoke from many kitchen stoves was curling lazily upwards into the sky.

After crossing through the mulberry grove, Old Tong Bao walked along the raised path between the paddy fields, then turned and looked again at that row of trees bursting with tender green buds. A twelve-year-old boy came bounding along from the other end of the fields, calling as he ran:

"Grandpa! Ma's waiting for you to come home and eat!"

It was Little Bao, Old Tong Bao's grandson.

"Coming!" the old man responded, still gazing at the mulberries. Only twice in his life had he seen these finger-like buds appear on the branches so soon after Clear and Bright. His family would probably have a fine crop of silkworms this year. Five trays of eggs

种,该可以采多少茧子呢? 只要不像去年,他家的债也许可以拔还一些罢。

小宝已经跑到他阿爹的身边了,也仰着脸看那绿绒似的桑拳头;忽然他跳起来拍着手唱道:

"清明削口,看蚕娘娘拍手!"

老通宝的皱脸上露出笑容来了。他觉得这是一个好兆头。他把手放在小宝的"和尚头"上摩着,他的被穷苦弄麻木了的老心里勃然又生出新的希望来了。

二

天气继续暖和,太阳光催开了那些桑拳头上的小手指儿模样的嫩叶,现在都有小小的手掌那么大了。老通宝他们那村庄四周围的桑林似乎发长得更好,远望去像一片绿锦平铺在密密层层灰白色矮矮的篱笆上。"希望"在老通宝和一般农民们的心里一点一点一天一天强大。蚕事的动员令也在各方

would hatch out a huge number of silkworms. If only they didn't have another bad market like last year, perhaps they could pay off part of their debt.

Little Bao stood beside his grandfather. The child too looked at the soft green on the gnarled fist branches. Jumping happily, he clapped his hands and chanted:

> *Green, tender leaves at Clear and Bright,*
> *The girls who tend silkworms*
> *Clap hands at the sight!*

The old man's wrinkled face broke into a smile. He thought it was a good omen for the little boy to respond like this on seeing the first buds of the year. He rubbed his hand affectionately over the child's shaven pate. In Old Tong Bao's heart, numbed wooden by a lifetime of poverty and hardship, suddenly hope began to stir again.

II

The weather remained warm. The rays of the sun forced open the tender, finger-like, little buds. They had already grown to the size of a small hand. Around Old Tong Bao's village, the mulberry trees seemed to respond especially well. From a distance they gave the appearance of a low grey picket fence on top of which a long swath of green brocade had been spread. Bit by bit, day by day, hope grew in the hearts of the villagers. The unspoken mobilization order for the silkworm

春蚕

面发动了。藏在柴房里一年之久的养蚕用具都拿出来洗刷修补。那条穿村而过的小溪旁边,蠕动着村里的女人和孩子,工作着,嚷着,笑着。

这些女人和孩子们都不是十分健康的脸色,——从今年开春起,他们都只吃个半饱;他们身上穿的,也只是些破旧的衣服。实在他们的情形比叫化子好不了多少。然而他们的精神都很不差。他们有很大的忍耐力,又有很大的幻想。虽然他们都负了天天在增大的债,可是他们那简单的头脑老是这么想:只要蚕花熟,就好了!他们想象到一个月以后那些绿油油的桑叶就会变成雪白的茧子,于是又变成丁丁当当响的洋钱,他们虽然肚子里饿得咕咕地叫,却也忍不住要笑。

这些女人中间也就有老通宝的媳妇四大娘和那个十二岁的小宝。这娘儿两个已经洗好了那些"团扁"和"蚕箪",坐在小溪边的石头上撩起布衫角揩脸上的汗水。

campaign reached everywhere and everyone. Silkworm rearing equipment that had been laid away for a year was again brought out to be scrubbed and mended. Beside the little stream which ran through the village, women and children, with much laughter and calling back and forth, washed the implements.

None of these women or children looked really healthy. Since the coming of spring, they had been eating only half their fill; their clothes were old and torn. As a matter of fact, they weren't much better off than beggars. Yet all were in quite good spirits, sustained by enormous patience and grand illusions. Burdened though they were by daily mounting debts, they had only one thought in their heads—If we get a good crop of silkworms, everything will be all right! . . . They could already visualize how, in a month, the shiny green leaves would be converted into snow-white cocoons, the cocoons exchanged for clinking silver dollars. Although their stomachs were growling with hunger, they couldn't refrain from smiling at this happy prospect.

Old Tong Bao's daughter-in-law was among the women by the stream. With the help of her twelve-year-old son, Little Pao, she had already finished washing the family's large trays of woven bamboo strips. Seated on a stone beside the stream, she wiped her perspiring face with the edge of her tunic. A twenty-year-old girl, working with other women on the op-

"四阿嫂！你们今年也看(养)洋种么？"

小溪对岸的一群女人中间有一个二十岁左右的姑娘隔溪喊过来了。四大娘认得是隔溪的对门邻舍陆福庆的妹子六宝。四大娘立刻把她的浓眉毛一挺，好像正想找人吵架似的嚷了起来：

"不要来问我！阿爹做主呢！——小宝的阿爹死不肯，只看了一张洋种！老糊涂的听得带一个洋字就好像见了七世冤家！洋钱，也是洋，他倒又要了！"

小溪旁那些女人们听得笑起来了。这时候有一个壮健的小伙子正从对岸的陆家稻场上走过，跑到溪边，跨上了那横在溪面用四根木头并排做成的雏形的"桥"。四大娘一眼看见，就丢开了"洋种"问题，高声喊道：

"多多弟！来帮我搬东西罢！这些扁，浸湿了，就像死狗一样重！"

小伙子阿多也不开口，走过来拿起五六只"团扁"，湿漉漉地顶在头上，却空着一双手，划桨似的荡着，就走了。这个阿多高兴起来时，什么事都肯做，碰到同村的女人们叫他帮忙拿什么重家伙，或是下溪去捞什么，他都肯；可是今天他大

posite side of the stream, hailed her:

"Are you raising foreign silkworms this year too?"

It was Sixth Treasure, sister of young Fu-ching, the neighbour who lived across the stream.

The thick eyebrows of Old Tong Bao's daughter-in-law at once contracted. Her voice sounded as if she had just been waiting for a chance to let off steam.

"Don't ask me; what the old man says, goes!" she shouted. "He's dead set against it, won't let us raise more than one batch of foreign breed! The old fool only has to hear the word 'foreign' to send him up in the air! He'll take dollars made of foreign silver, though; those are the only 'foreign' things he likes!"

The women on the other side of the stream laughed. From the threshing ground behind them a strapping young man approached. He reached the stream and crossed over on the four logs that served as a bridge. Seeing him, his sister-in-law dropped her tirade and called in a high voice:

"Ah Duo, will you help me carry these trays? They're as heavy as dead dogs when they're wet!"

Without a word, Ah Duo lifted the six big trays and set them, dripping, on his head. Balancing them in place, he walked off, swinging his hands in a swimming motion. When in a good mood, Ah Duo refused nobody. If any of the village women asked him to carry something heavy or fish something out of the stream, he was usually quite willing. But today he probably was a

161

概有点不高兴,所以只顶了五六只"团扁"去,却空着一双手。那些女人们看着他戴了那特别大箬帽似的一叠"扁",袅着腰,学镇上女人的样子走着,又都笑起来了。老通宝家紧邻的李根生的老婆荷花一边笑,一边叫道:

"喂,多多头!回来!也替我带一点儿去!"

"叫我一声好听的,我就给你拿。"

阿多也笑着回答,仍然走。转眼间就到了他家的廊下,就把头上的"团扁"放在廊檐口。

"那么,叫你一声干儿子!"

荷花说着就大声的笑起来,她那出众地白净然而扁得作怪的脸上看去就好像只有一张大嘴和眯紧了好像两条线一般的细眼睛。她原是镇上人家的婢女,嫁给那不声不响整天苦着脸的半老头子李根生还不满半年,可是她的爱和男子们胡调已经在村中很有名。

"不要脸的!"

忽然对岸那群女人中间有人轻声骂了一句。荷花的那对细眼睛立刻睁大了,怒声嚷道:

"骂哪一个?有本事,当面

little grumpy, and so he walked empty-handed with only six trays on his head. The sight of him, looking as if he were wearing six layers of wide straw hats, his waist twisting at each step in imitation of the ladies of the town, sent the women into peals of laughter. Lotus, wife of Old Tong Bao's nearest neighbour, called with a giggle:

"Hey, Ah Duo, come back here. Carry a few trays for me too!"

Ah Duo grinned. "Not unless you call me a sweet name!" He continued walking. An instant later he had reached the porch of his house and set down the trays out of the sun.

"Will 'kid brother' do?" demanded Lotus, laughing boisterously. She had a remarkably clean white complexion, but her face was very flat. When she laughed, all that could be seen was a big open mouth and two tiny slits of eyes. Originally a slavey in a house in town, she had been married off to Old Tong Bao's neighbour—a prematurely aged man who walked around with a sour expression and never said a word all day. That was less than six months ago, but her love affairs and escapades already were the talk of the village.

"Shameless hussy!" came a contemptuous female voice from across the stream.

Lotus' piggy eyes immediately widened. "Who said that?" she demanded angrily. "If you've got the

骂,不要躲!"

"你管得我?棺材横头踢一脚,死人肚里自得知:我就骂那不要脸的骚货!"

隔溪立刻回骂过来了,这就是那六宝,又一位村里有名淘气的大姑娘。

于是对骂之下,两边又泼水。爱闹的女人也夹在中间帮这边帮那边。小孩子们笑着狂呼。四大娘是老成的,提起她的"蚕箪",喊着小宝,自回家去。阿多站在廊下看着笑。他知道为什么六宝要跟荷花吵架;他看着那"辣货"六宝挨骂,倒觉得很高兴。

老通宝掮着一架"蚕台"从屋子里出来。这三棱形家伙的木梗子有几条给白蚂蚁蛀过了,怕的不牢,须得修补一下。看见阿多站在那里笑嘻嘻地望着外边的女人们吵架,老通宝的脸色就板起来了。他这"多多头"的小儿子不老成,他知道。尤其使他不高兴的,是多多也和紧邻的荷花说说笑笑。"那母狗是白虎星,惹上了她就得败家",——老通宝时常这样警戒他的小儿子。

brass to call me names, let's see you try in to my face! Come out into the open!"

"Think you can handle me? I'm talking about a shameless, man-crazy baggage! If the shoe fits, wear it!" retorted Sixth Treasure, for it was she who had spoken. She too was famous in the village, but as a mischievous, lively young woman.

The two began splashing water at each other from opposite banks of the stream. Girls who enjoyed a row took sides and joined the battle, while the children whooped with laughter. Old Tong Bao's daughter-in-law was more decorous. She picked up her remaining trays, called to Little Bao and returned home. Ah Duo watched from the porch, grinning. He knew why Sixth Treasure and Lotus were quarrelling. It did his heart good to hear that sharp-tongued Sixth Treasure get told off in public.

Old Tong Bao came out of the house with a wooden traystand on his shoulder. Some of the legs of the uprights had been eaten by termites, and he wanted to repair them. At the sight of Ah Duo standing there laughing at the women, Old Tong Bao's face lengthened. The boy hadn't much sense of propriety, he well knew. What disturbed him particularly was the way Ah Duo and Lotus were always talking and laughing together. "That bitch is an evil spirit. Fooling with her will bring ruin on our house," he had often warned his younger son.

春蚕

"阿多!空手看野景么?阿四在后边扎'缀头',你去帮他!"

老通宝像一匹疯狗似的咆哮着,火红的眼睛一直盯住了阿多的身体,直到阿多走进屋里去,看不见了,老通宝方缠提过那"蚕台"来反复审察,慢慢地动手修补。木匠生活,老通宝早年是会的;但近来他老了,手指头没有劲,他修了一会儿,抬起头来喘气,又望望屋里挂在竹竿上的三张蚕种。

四大娘就在廊檐口糊"蚕箪"。去年他们为的想省几百文钱,是买了旧报纸来糊的。老通宝直到现在还说是因为用了报纸——不惜字纸,所以去年他们的蚕花不好。今年是特地全家少吃一餐饭,省下钱来买了"糊箪纸"来了。四大娘把那鹅黄色坚韧的纸儿糊得很平贴,然后又照品字式糊上三张小小的花纸——那是跟"糊箪纸"一块儿买来的,一张印的花色是"聚宝盆",另两张都是手执尖角旗的人儿骑在马上,据

"Ah Duo!" he now barked angrily. "Enjoying the scenery? Your brother's in the back mending equipment. Go and give him a hand!" His inflamed eyes bored into Ah Duo, never leaving the boy until he disappeared into the house.

Only then did Old Tong Bao start work on the tray-stand. After examining it carefully, he slowly began his repairs. Years ago, Old Tong Bao had worked for a time as a carpenter. But he was old now; his fingers had lost their strength. A few minutes' work and he was breathing hard. He raised his head and looked into the house. Five squares of cloth to which sticky silkworm eggs were adhered, hung from a horizontal bamboo pole.

His daughter-in-law, Ah Si's wife, was at the other end of the porch, pasting paper on big trays of woven bamboo strips. Last year. to economize a bit, they had bought and used old newspaper. Old Tong Bao still maintained that was why the eggs had hatched poorly—it was unlucky to use paper with writing on it for such a prosaic purpose. Writing meant scholarship, and scholarship had to be respected. This year the whole family had skipped a meal and with the money saved, purchased special "tray pasting paper." Ah Si's wife pasted the tough, gosling-yellow sheets smooth and flat; on every tray she also affixed three little coloured paper pictures, bought at the same time. One was the "Platter of Plenty"; the other two showed a militant fig-

说是"蚕花太子"。

"四大娘！你爸爸做中人借来三十块钱,就只买了二十担叶。后天米又吃完了,怎么办？"

老通宝气喘喘地从他的工作里抬起头来,望着四大娘。那三十块钱是二分半的月息。总算有四大娘的父亲张财发做中人,那债主也就是张财发的东家"做好事",这才只要了二分半的月息。条件是蚕事完后本利归清。

四大娘把糊好了的"蚕箪"放在太阳底下晒,好像生气似的说：

"都买了叶！又像去年那样多下来——"

"什么话！你倒先来发利市了！年年像去年么？自家只有十来担叶；五张布子（蚕种）,十来担叶够么？"

"噢,噢；你总是不错的！我只晓得有米烧饭,没米饿肚子！"

四大娘气哄哄地回答；为了那"洋种"问题,她到现在常

168

ure on horseback, pennant in hand. He, according to local belief, was the "Guardian of Silkworm Hatching."

"I was only able to buy twenty loads of mulberry leaves with that thirty silver dollars I borrowed on your father's guarantee," Old Tong Bao said to his daughter-in-law. He was still panting from his exertions with the tray-stand. "Our rice will be finished by the day after tomorrow. What are we going to do?"

Thanks to her father's influence with his boss and his willingness to guarantee repayment of the loan, Old Tong Bao was able to borrow the money at a low rate of interest—only twenty-five per cent a month! Both the principal and interest had to be repaid by the end of the silkworm season.

Ah Si's wife finished pasting a tray and placed it in the sun. "You've spent it all on leaves," she said angrily. "We'll have a lot of leaves left over, just like last year!"

"Full of lucky words, aren't you?" demanded the old man, sarcastically. "I suppose every year'll be like last year? We can't get more than a dozen or so loads of leaves from our own trees. With five sets of grubs to feed, that won't be nearly enough."

"Oh, of course, you're never wrong!" she replied hotly. "All I know is with rice we can eat, without it we'll go hungry!" His stubborn refusal to raise any foreign silkworms last year had left them with only the un-

要和老通宝抬杠。

老通宝气得脸都紫了。两个人就此再没有一句话。

但是"收蚕"的时期一天一天逼近了。这二三十人家的小村落突然呈现了一种大紧张,大决心,大奋斗,同时又是大希望。人们似乎连肚子饿都忘记了。老通宝他们家东借一点,西赊一点,居然也一天一天过着来。也不仅老通宝他们,村里哪一家有两三斗米放在家里呀!去年秋收固然还好,可是地主、债主、正税、杂捐,一层一层地剥削来,早就完了。现在他们唯一的指望就是春蚕,一切临时借贷都是指明在这"春蚕收成"中偿还。

他们都怀着十分希望又十分恐惧的心情来准备这春蚕的大搏战!

"谷雨"节一天近一天了。村里二三十人家的"布子"都隐隐现出绿色来。女人们在稻场上碰见时,都匆匆地带着焦灼

salable local breed. As a result, she was often contrary with him.

The old man's face turned purple with rage. After this, neither would speak to the other.

But hatching time was drawing closer every day. The little village's two dozen families were thrown into a state of great tension, great determination, great struggle. With it all, they were possessed of a great hope, a hope that could almost make them forget their hungry bellies.

Old Tong Bao's family, borrowing a little here, getting a little credit there, somehow managed to get by. Nor did the other families eat any better; there wasn't one with a spare bag of rice! Although they had harvested a good crop the previous year, landlords, creditors, taxes, levies, one after another, had cleaned the peasants out long ago. Now all their hopes were pinned on the spring silkworms. The repayment date of every loan they made was set for the "end of the silkworm season."

With high hopes and considerable fear, like soldiers going into a hand-to-hand battle to the death, they prepared for their spring silkworm campaign!

"Grain Rain" day—bringing gentle drizzles—was not far off. Almost imperceptibly, the silkworm eggs of the two dozen village families began to show faint tinges of green. Women, when they met on the public threshing ground, would speak to one another agitatedly in

而快乐的口气互相告诉道：

"六宝家快要'窝种'了呀！"

"荷花说她家明天就要'窝'了。有这么快！"

"黄道士去侧一字，今年的青叶要贵到四洋！"

四大娘看自家的五张"布子"。不对！那黑芝麻似的一片细点子还是黑沉沉，不见绿影。她的丈夫阿四拿到亮处去细看，也找不出几点"绿"来。四大娘很着急。

"你就先'窝'起来罢！这余杭种，作兴是慢一点的。"

阿四看着他老婆，勉强自家宽慰。四大娘堵起了嘴巴不回答。

老通宝哭丧着干皱的老脸，没说什么，心里却觉得不妙。

幸而再过了一天，四大娘再细心看那"布子"时，哈，有几处转成绿色了！而且绿的很有光彩。四大娘立刻告诉了丈夫，告诉了老通宝，多多头，也告诉了她的儿子小宝。她就把那些布子贴肉揾在胸前，抱着

tones that were anxious yet joyful.

"Over at Sixth Treasure's place, they're almost ready to incubate their eggs!"

"Lotus says her family is going to start incubating tomorrow. So soon!"

"Huang 'the Priest' has made a divination. He predicts that this spring mulberry leaves will go to four dollars a load!"

Old Tong Bao's daughter-in-law examined their five sets of eggs. They looked bad. The tiny seed-like eggs were still pitch black, without even a hint of green. Her husband, Ah Si, took them into the light to peer at them carefully. Even so, he could find hardly any ripening eggs. She was very worried.

"You incubate them anyhow. Maybe this variety is a little slow," her husband forced himself to say consolingly.

Her lips pressed tight, she made no reply.

Old Tong Bao's wrinkled face sagged with dejection. Though he said nothing, he thought their prospects were dim.

The next day, Ah Si's wife again examined the eggs. Ha! Quite a few were turning green, and a very shiny green at that! Immediately, she told her husband, told Old Tong Bao, Ah Duo...she even told her son Little Bao. Now the incubating process could begin! She held the five pieces of cloth to which the eggs were adhered against her bare bosom. As if cuddling a

吃奶的婴孩似的静静儿坐着,动也不敢多动了。夜间,她抱着那五张布子到被窝里,把阿四赶去和多多头做一床。那布子上密密麻麻的蚕子儿贴着肉,怪痒痒的;四大娘很快活,又有点儿害怕,她第一次怀孕时胎儿在肚子里动,她也是那样半惊半喜的!

全家都是惴惴不安地又很兴奋地等候"收蚕"。只有多多头例外。他说:今年蚕花一定好,可是想发财却是命里不曾来。老通宝骂他多嘴,他还是要说。

蚕房早已收拾好了。"窝种"的第二天,老通宝拿一个大蒜头涂上一些泥,放在蚕房的墙脚边;这也是年年的惯例,但今番老通宝更加虔诚,手也抖了。去年他们"卜"的非常灵验。可是去年那"灵验",现在老通宝想也不敢想。

现在这村里家家都在"窝种"了。稻场上和小溪边顿时少了那些女人们的踪迹。一个"戒严令"也在无形中颁布了;乡农们即使平日是最好的,也不往来;人客来冲了蚕神不是

nursing infant, she sat absolutely quiet, not daring to stir. At night, she took the five sets to bed with her. Her husband was routed out, and had to share Ah Duo's bed. The tiny silkworm eggs were very scratchy against her flesh. She felt happy and a little frightened, like the first time she was pregnant and the baby moved inside her. Exactly the same sensation!

Uneasy but eager, the whole family waited for the eggs to hatch. Ah Duo was the only exception. We're sure to hatch a good crop, he said, but anyone who thinks we're going to get rich in this life, is out of his head. Though the old man swore Ah Duo's big mouth would ruin their luck, the boy stuck to his guns.

A clean dry shed for the growing grubs was all prepared. The second day of incubation, Old Tong Bao smeared a garlic with earth and placed it at the foot of the wall inside the shed. If, in a few days, the garlic put out many sprouts, it meant the eggs would hatch well. He did this every year, but this year he was more reverential than usual, and his hands trembled. Last year's divination had proved all too accurate. He didn't dare to think about that now.

Every family in the village was busy "incubating." For the time being there were few women's footprints on the threshing ground or the banks of the little stream. An unofficial "martial law" had been imposed. Even peasants normally on very good terms stopped visiting one another. For a guest to come and frighten

玩的！他们至多在稻场上低声交谈一二句就走开。这是个"神圣"的季节。

老通宝家的五张布子上也有些"乌娘"蠕蠕地动了。于是全家的空气，突然紧张。那正是"谷雨"前一日。四大娘料来可以挨过了"谷雨"节那一天。布子不须再"窝"了，很小心地放在"蚕房"里。老通宝偷眼看一下那个躺在墙脚边的大蒜头，他心里就一跳。那大蒜头上还只有一两茎绿芽！老通宝不敢再看，心里祷祝后天正午会有更多更多的绿芽。

终于"收蚕"的日子到了。四大娘心神不定地淘米烧饭，时时看饭锅上的热气有没有直冲上来。老通宝拿出预先买了来的香烛点起来，恭恭敬敬放在灶君神位前。阿四和阿多去到田里采野花。小小宝帮着把灯芯草剪成细末子，又把采来的野花揉碎。一切都准备齐全了时，太阳也近午刻了，饭锅上

away the spirits of the ripening eggs—that would be no laughing matter! At most, people exchanged a few words in low tones when they met, then quickly separated. This was the "sacred" season!

Old Tong Bao's family was on pins and needles. In the five sets of eggs a few grubs had begun wriggling. It was exactly one day before Grain Rain. Ah Si's wife had calculated that most of the eggs wouldn't hatch until after that day. Before or after Grain Rain was all right, but for eggs to hatch on the day itself was considered highly unlucky. Incubation was no longer necessary, and the eggs were carefully placed in the special shed. Old Tong Bao stole a glance at his garlic at the foot of the wall. His heart dropped. There were still only the same two small green shoots the garlic had originally! He didn't dare to look any closer. He prayed silently that by noon the day after tomorrow the garlic would have many, many more shoots.

At last hatching day arrived. Ah Si's wife set a pot of rice on to boil and nervously watched for the time when the steam from it would rise straight up. Old Tong Bao lit the incense and candles he had bought in anticipation of this event. Devoutly, he placed them before the idol of the Kitchen God. His two sons went into the fields to pick wild flowers. Little Bao chopped a lamp-wick into fine pieces and crushed the wild flowers the men brought back. Everything was ready. The sun was entering its zenith; steam from the rice pot

177

春蚕

水蒸气嘟嘟地直冲,四大娘立刻跳了起来,把"蚕花"和一对鹅毛插在发髻上,就到"蚕房"里。老通宝拿着秤杆,阿四拿了那揉碎的野花片儿和灯芯草碎末。四大娘揭开"布分",就从阿四手里拿过那野花碎片和灯芯草末子撒在"布子"上,又接过老通宝手里的秤杆来,将"布子"挽在秤杆上,于是拔下发髻上的鹅毛在布子上轻轻儿拂;野花片,灯芯草末子,连同"乌娘",都拂在那"蚕箪"里了。一张,两张,……都拂过了;最后一张是洋种,那就收在另一个"蚕箪"里。末了,四大娘又拔下发髻上那朵"蚕花",跟鹅毛一块插在"蚕箪"的边儿上。

这是一个隆重的仪式!千百年相传的仪式!那好比是誓师典礼,以后就要开始了一个月光景的和恶劣的天气和恶运以及和不知什么的连日连夜无休息的大决战!

"乌娘"在"蚕箪"里蠕动,样子非常强健;那黑色也是很正路的。四大娘和老通宝他们都放心地松一口气了。但当老

puffed straight upwards. Ah Si's wife immediately leaped to her feet, stuck a "sacred" paper flower and a pair of goose feathers into the knot of hair at the back of her head and went to the shed. Old Tong Bao carried a wooden scale-pole; Ah Si followed with the chopped lamp-wick and the crushed wild flowers. Daughter-in-law uncovered the cloth pieces to which the grubs were adhered, and sprinkled them with the bits of wick and flowers Ah Si was holding. Then she took the wooden scale-pole from Old Tong Bao and hung the cloth pieces over it. She next removed the pair of goose feathers from her hair. Moving them lightly across the cloth, she brushed the grubs, together with the crushed lampwick and wild flowers, on to a large tray. One set, two sets... the last set contained the foreign breed. The grubs from this cloth were brushed on to a separate tray. Finally, she removed the "sacred" paper flower from her hair and pinned it, with the "goose feathers, against the side of the tray.

A solemn ceremony! One that had been handed down through the ages! Like warriors taking an oath before going into battle! Old Tong Bao and family now had ahead of them a month of fierce combat, with no rest day or night, against bad weather, bad luck and anything else that might come along!

The grubs, wriggling in the trays, looked very healthy. They were all the proper black colour. Old Tong Bao and his daughter-in-law were able to relax a

通宝悄悄地把那个"命运"的大蒜头拿起来看时,他的脸色立刻变了!大蒜头上还只得三四茎嫩芽!天哪!难道又同去年一样?

三

然而那"命运"的大蒜头这次竟不灵验。老通宝家的蚕非常好!虽然头眠二眠的时候连天阴雨,气候是比"清明"边似乎还要冷一点,可是那些"宝宝"都很强健。

村里别人家的"宝宝"也都不差。紧张的快乐弥漫了全村庄,似那小溪里琮琮的流水也像是朗朗的笑声了。只有荷花家是例外。她们家看了一张"布子",可是"出火"只称得二十斤;"大眠"快边人们还看见那不声不响晦气色的丈夫根生倾弃了三"蚕箪"在那小溪里。

这一件事,使得全村的妇人对于荷花家特别"戒严"。她们特地避路,不从荷花的门前走,远远的看见了荷花或是她那不声不响丈夫的影儿就赶快躲开;这些幸运的人儿惟恐看了荷花他们一眼或是交谈半句

little. But when the old man secretly took another look at his garlic, he turned pale! It had grown only four measly shoots! Ah! Would this year be like last year all over again?

III

But the "fateful" garlic proved to be not so psychic after all. The silkworms of Old Tong Bao's family grew and thrived! Though it rained continuously during the grubs' First Sleep and Second Sleep, and the weather was a bit colder than at Clear and Bright, the "little darlings" were extremely robust.

The silkworms of the other families in the village were not doing badly either. A tense kind of joy pervaded the countryside. Even the small stream seemed to be gurgling with bright laughter. Lotus' family was the sole exception. They were only raising one set of grubs, but by the Third Sleep their silkworms weighed less than twenty catties. Just before the Big Sleep, people saw Lotus' husband walk to the stream and dump out his trays. That dour, old-looking man had bad luck written all over him.

Because of this dreadful event, the village women put Lotus' family strictly "off limits." They made wide detours so as not to pass her door. If they saw her or her taciturn husband, no matter how far away, they made haste to go in the opposite direction. They feared that even one look at Lotus or her spouse, the briefest

话就传染了晦气来！

老通宝严禁他的小儿子多多头跟荷花说话。——"你再跟那东西多嘴，我就告你忤逆！"老通宝站在廊檐外高声大气喊，故意要叫荷花他们听得。

小小宝也受到严厉的嘱咐，不许跑到荷花家的门前，不许和他们说话。

阿多像一个聋子似的不理睬老头子那早早夜夜的唠叨，他心里却在暗笑。全家就只有他不大相信那些鬼禁忌。可是他也没有跟荷花说话，他忙都忙不过来。

"大眠"捉了毛三百斤，老通宝全家连十二岁的小宝也在内，都是两日两夜没有合眼。蚕是少见的好，活了六十岁的老通宝记得只有两次是同样的，一次就是他成家的那年，又一次是阿四出世那一年。"大眠"以后的"宝宝"第一天就吃了七担叶，个个是生青滚壮，然而老通宝全家都瘦了一圈，失眠的眼睛上布满了红丝。

谁也料得到这些"宝宝"上

conversation, would contaminate them with the unfortunate couple's bad luck!

Old Tong Bao strictly forbade Ah Duo to talk to Lotus. "If I catch you gabbing with that baggage again, I'll disown you!" he threatened in a loud, angry voice, standing outside on the porch to make sure Lotus could hear him.

Little Bao was also warned not to play in front of Lotus' door, and not to speak to anyone in her family.

The old man harped at Ah Duo morning, noon and night, but the boy turned a deaf ear to his father's grumbling. In his heart, he laughed at it. Of the whole family, Ah Duo alone didn't place much stock in taboos and superstitions. He didn't talk with Lotus, however. He was much too busy for that.

By the Big Sleep, their silkworms weighed three hundred catties. Every member of Old Tong Bao's family, including twelve-year-old Little Bao, worked for two days and two nights without sleeping a wink. The silkworms were unusually sturdy. Only twice in his sixty years had Old Tong Bao ever seen the like. Once was the year he married; once when his first son was born.

The first day after the Big Sleep, the "little darlings" ate seven loads of leaves. They were now a bright green, thick and healthy. Old Tong Bao and his family, on the contrary, were much thinner, their eyes bloodshot from lack of sleep.

No one could guess how much the "little darlings"

山前还得吃多少叶。老通宝和儿子阿四商量了：

"陈大少爷借不出，还是再求财发的东家罢？"

"地头上还有十担叶，够一天。"

阿四回答，他委实是支撑不住了，他的一双眼皮像有几百斤重，只想合下来。老通宝却不耐烦了，怒声喝道：

"说什么梦话！刚吃了两天老蚕呢。明天不算，还得吃三天，还要三十担叶，三十担！"

这时外边稻场上忽然人声喧闹，阿多押了新发来的五担叶来了。于是老通宝和阿四的谈话打断，都出去"抒叶"。四大娘也慌忙从蚕房里钻出来。隔溪陆家养的蚕不多，那大姑娘六宝抽得出工夫，也来帮忙了。那时星光满天，微微有点风，村前村后都断断续续传来了吆喝和欢笑，中间有一个粗暴的声音嚷道：

"叶行情飞涨了！今天下午镇上开到四洋一担！"

老通宝偏偏听得了，心里急得什么似的。四块钱一担，三十担可要一百二十块呢，他哪来这许多钱！但是想到茧子

would eat before they spun their cocoons. Old Tong Bao discussed the question of buying more leaves with Ah Si.

"Master Chen won't lend us any more. Shall we try your father-in-law's boss again?"

"We've still got ten loads coming. That's enough for one more day," replied Ah Si. He could barely hold himself erect. His eyelids weighed a thousand catties. They kept wanting to close.

"One more day? You're dreaming!" snapped the old man impatiently. "Not counting tomorrow, they still have to eat three more days. We'll need another thirty loads! Thirty loads, I say!"

Loud voices were heard outside on the threshing ground. Ah Duo had arrived with men delivering five loads of mulberry branches. Everyone went out to strip the leaves. Ah Si's wife hurried from the shed. Across the stream, Sixth Treasure and her family were raising only a small crop of silkworms; having spare time, she came over to help. Bright stars filled the sky. There was a slight wind. All up and down the village, gay shouts and laughter rang in the night.

"The price of leaves is rising fast!" a coarse voice cried. "This afternoon, they were getting four dollars a load in the market town!"

Old Tong Bao was very upset. At four dollars a load, thirty loads would come to a hundred and twenty dollars. Where could he raise so much money! But

总可以采五百多斤,就算五十块钱一百斤,也有这么二百五,他又心里一宽。那边"捋叶"的人堆里忽然又有一个小小的声音说:

"听说东路不大好,看来叶价钱涨不到多少的!"

老通宝认得这声音是陆家的六宝。这使他心里又一宽。

那六宝是和阿多同站在一个筐子边"捋叶"。在半明半暗的星光下,她和阿多靠得很近。忽然她觉得在那"杠条"的隐蔽下,有一只手在她大腿上拧了一把。好像知道是谁拧的,她忍住了不笑,也不声张。蓦地那手又在她胸前摸了一把,六宝直跳起来,出惊地喊了一声:

"嗳哟!"

"什么事?"

同在那筐子边捋叶的四大娘问了,抬起头来。六宝觉得自己脸上热烘烘了,她偷偷地瞪了阿多一眼,就赶快低下头,很快地捋叶,一面回答:

"没有什么。想来是毛毛虫刺了我一下。"

阿多咬住了嘴唇暗笑。虽然在这半个月来也是半饱而且少睡,也瘦了许多了,他的精神

then he figured—he was sure to gather over five hundred catties of cocoons. Even at fifty dollars a hundred, they'd sell for two hundred and fifty dollars. Feeling a bit consoled, he heard a small voice from among the leaf-strippers.

"They say the folks east of here aren't doing so well with their silkworms. There won't be any reason for the price of leaves to go much higher."

Old Tong Bao recognized the speaker as Sixth Treasure, and he relaxed still further.

The girl and Ah Duo were standing beside a large basket, stripping leaves. In the dim starlight, they worked quite close to each other, partly hidden by the pile of mulberry branches before them. Suddenly, Sixth Treasure felt someone pinch her thigh. She knew well enough who it was, and she suppressed a giggle. But when, a moment later, a hand brushed against her breasts, she jumped; a little shriek escaped her.

"Aiya!"

"What's wrong?" demanded Ah Si's wife, working on the other side of the basket.

Sixth Treasure's face flamed scarlet. She shot a glance at Ah Duo, then quickly lowered her head and resumed stripping leaves. "Nothing," she replied. "I think a caterpillar bit me!"

Ah Duo bit his lips to keep from laughing aloud. He had been half starved the past two weeks and had slept little. But in spite of having lost a lot of weight,

可还是很饱满。老通宝那种忧愁,他是永远没有的。他永不相信靠一次蚕花好或是田里熟,他们就可以还清了债再有自己的田;他知道单靠勤俭工作,即使做到背脊骨折断也是不能翻身的。但是他仍旧很高兴地工作着,他觉得这也是一种快活,正像和六宝调情一样。

第二天早上,老通宝就到镇里去想法借钱来买叶。临走前,他和四大娘商量好,决定把他家那块出产十五担叶的桑地去抵押。这是他家最后的产业。

叶又买来了三十担。第一批的十担发来时,那些壮健的"宝宝"已经饿了半点钟了。"宝宝"们尖出了小嘴巴,向左向右乱撮,四大娘看得心酸。叶铺了上去,立刻蚕房里充满着萨萨萨的响声,人们说话也不大听得清。不多一会儿,那些"团扁"里立刻又全见白了,于是又铺上厚厚的一层叶。人们单是"上叶"也就忙得透不过

he was in high spirits. While he never suffered from any of Old Tong Bao's gloom, neither did he believe that one good crop, whether of silkworms or of rice, would enable them to wipe off their debt and own their own land again. He knew they would never "get out from under" merely by relying on hard work, even if they broke their backs trying. Nevertheless, he worked with a will. He enjoyed work, just as he enjoyed fooling around with Sixth Treasure.

The next morning, Old Tong Bao went into town to borrow money for more leaves. Before leaving home, he had talked the matter over with daughter-in-law. They had decided to mortgage their grove of mulberries that produced fifteen loads of leaves a year as security for the loan. The grove was the last piece of property the family owned.

By the time the old man ordered another thirty loads, and the first ten were delivered, the sturdy "little darlings" had gone hungry for half an hour. Putting forth their pointed little mouths, they swayed from side to side, searching for food. Daughter-in-law's heart had ached to see them. When the leaves were finally spread in the trays, the silkworm shed at once resounded with a sibilant crunching, so noisy it drowned out conversation. In a very short while, the trays were again empty of leaves. Another thick layer was piled on. Just keeping the silkworms supplied with leaves, Old Tong Bao and his family were so busy they could barely catch

气来。但这是最后五分钟了。再得两天,"宝宝"可以上山。人们把剩余的精力榨出来拼死命干。

　　阿多虽然接连三日三夜没有睡,却还不见怎么倦。那一夜,就由他一个人在"蚕房"里守那上半夜,好让老通宝以及阿四夫妇都去歇一歇。那是个好月夜,稍稍有点冷。蚕房里煨了一个小小的火。阿多守到二更过,上了第二次的叶,就蹲在那个"火"旁边听那些"宝宝"萨萨萨地吃叶。渐渐儿他的眼皮合上了。恍惚听得有门响,阿多的眼皮一跳,睁开眼来看了看,就又合上了。他耳朵里还听得萨萨萨的声音和屑索屑索的怪声。猛然一个踉跄,他的头在自己膝头上磕了一下,他惊醒过来,恰就听得蚕房的芦帘拍叉一声响,似乎还看见有人影一闪。阿多立刻跳起来,到外面一看,门是开着,月光下稻场上有一个人正走向溪边去。阿多飞也似跳出去,还没看清那人是谁,已经把那人抓过来摔在地下。他断定了这是一个贼。

　　"多多头!打死我也不怨你,只求你不要说出来!"

　　是荷花的声音,阿多听真了时不禁浑身的汗毛都竖了起

their breath. But this was the final crisis. In two more days the "little darlings" would spin their cocoons. People were putting every bit of their remaining strength into this last desperate struggle.

Though he had gone without sleep for three whole days, Ah Duo didn't appear particularly tired. He agreed to watch the shed alone that night until dawn to permit the others to get some rest. There was a bright moon and the weather was a trifle cold. Ah Duo crouched beside a small fire he had built in the shed. At about eleven, he gave the silkworms their second feeding, then returned to squat by the fire. He could hear the loud rustle of the "little darlings" crunching through the leaves. His eyes closed. Suddenly, he heard the door squeak, and his eyelids flew open. He peered into the darkness for a moment, then shut his eyes again. His ears were still hissing with the rustle of the leaves. The next thing he knew, his head had struck against his knees. Waking with a start, he heard the door screen bang and thought he saw a moving shadow. Ah Duo leaped up and rushed outside. In the moonlight, he saw somcone crossing the threshing ground towards the stream. He caught up in a flash, seized and flung the intruder to the ground. Ah Duo was sure he had nabbed a thief.

"Ah Duo, kill me if you want to, but don't give me away!"

The voice made Ah Duo's hair stand on end. He

来。月光下他又看见那扁得作怪的白脸儿上一对细圆的眼睛定定地看住了他。可是恐怖的意思那眼睛里也没有。阿多哼了一声,就问道:

"你偷什么?"

"我偷你们的宝宝!"

"放到哪里去了?"

"我扔到溪里去了!"

阿多现在也变了脸色。他这才知道这女人的恶意是要冲克他家的"宝宝"。

"你真心毒呀!我们家和你们可没有冤仇!"

"没有么?有的,有的!我家自管蚕花不好,可并没害了谁,你们都是好的!你们怎么把我当作白老虎,远远地望见我就别转了脸?你们不把我当人看待!"

那妇人说着就爬了起来,脸上的神气比什么都可怕。阿多瞅着那妇人好半晌,这才说道:

"我不打你,走你的罢!"

阿多头也不回的跑回家去,仍在"蚕房"里守着。他完全没有睡意了。他看那些"宝宝",都是好好的。他并没想到荷花可恨或可怜,然而他不能忘记荷花那一番话;他觉到人和人中间有什么地方是永远弄不对的,可是他不能够明白想

could see in the moonlight that queer flat white face and those round little piggy eyes fixed upon him. But of menace, the piggy eyes had none. Ah Duo snorted.

"What were you after?"

"A few of your family's little darlings'!"

"What did you do with them?"

"Threw them in the stream!"

Ah Duo's face darkened. He knew that in this way she was trying to put a curse on the lot. "You're pure poison! We never did anything to hurt you."

"Never did anything? Oh yes, you did! Yes, you did! Our silkworm eggs didn't hatch well, but we didn't harm anybody. You were all so smart! You shunned me like a leper. No matter how far away I was, if you saw me, you turned your heads. You acted as if I wasn't even human!"

She got to her feet, the agonized expression on her face terrible to see. Ah Duo stared at her. "I'm not going to beat you," he said finally. "Go on your way!"

Without giving her another glance, he trotted back to the shed. He was wide awake now. Lotus had only taken a handful and the remaining "little darlings" were all in good condition. It didn't occur to him either to hate or pity Lotus, but the last thing she had said remained in his mind. It seemed to him there was something eternally wrong in the scheme of human relations; but he couldn't put his finger on what it was ex-

193

出来是什么地方,或是为什么。再过一会儿,他就什么都忘记了。"宝宝"是强健的,像有魔法似的吃了又吃,永远不会饱!

以后直到东方快打白了时,没有发生事故。老通宝和四大娘来替换阿多了,他们拿那些渐渐身体发白而变短了的"宝宝"在亮处照着,看是"有没有通"。他们的心被快活胀大了。但是太阳出山时四大娘到溪边汲水,却看见六宝满脸严重地跑过来悄悄地问道:

"昨夜二更过,三更不到,我远远地看见那骚货从你们家跑出来,阿多跟在后面,他们站在这里说了半天话呢!四阿嫂!你们怎么不管事呀?"

四大娘的脸色立刻变了,一句话也没说,提了水桶就回家去,先对丈夫说了,再对老通宝说。这东西竟偷进人家"蚕房"来了,那还了得!老通宝气得直跺脚,马上叫了阿多来查问。但是阿多不承认,说六宝是做梦见鬼。老通宝又去找六宝询问。六宝是一口咬定了看

catly, nor did he know why it should be. In a little while, he forgot about this too. The lusty silkworms were eating and eating, yet, as if by some magic, never full!

Nothing more happened that night. Just before the sky began to brighten in the east, Old Tong Bao and his daughter-in-law came to relieve Ah Duo. They took the trays of "little darlings" and looked at them in the light. The silkworms were turning a whiter colour, their bodies gradually becoming shorter and thicker. They were delighted with the excellent way the silkworms were developing.

But when, at sunrise, Ah Si's wife went to draw water at the stream, she met Sixth Treasure. The girl's expression was serious.

"I saw that slut leaving your place shortly before midnight," she whispered. "Ah Duo was right behind her. They stood here and talked for a long time! Your family ought to look after things better than that!"

The colour drained from the face of Ah Si's wife. Without a word, she carried her water bucket back to the house. First she told her husband about it, then she told Old Tong Bao. It was a fine state of affairs when a baggage like that could sneak into people's silkworm sheds! Old Tong Bao stamped with rage. He immediately summoned Ah Duo. But the boy denied the whole story; he said Sixth Treasure was dreaming. The old man then went to question Sixth Treasure. She in-

见的。老通宝没有主意,回家去看那"宝宝",仍然是很健康,瞧不出一些败相来。

但是老通宝他们满心的欢喜却被这件事打消了。他们相信六宝的话不会毫无根据。他们唯一的希望是那骚货或者只在廊檐口和阿多鬼混了一阵。

"可是那大蒜头上的苗却当真只有三四茎呀!"

老通宝自心里这么想,觉得前途只是阴暗。可不是,吃了许多叶去,一直落来都很好,然而上了山却干僵了的事,也是常有的。不过老通宝无论如何不敢想到这上头去;他以为即使是肚子里想,也是不吉利。

四

"宝宝"都上山了,老通宝他们还是捏着一把汗。他们钱都花光了,精力也绞尽了,可是有没有报酬呢,到此时还没有把握。虽则如此,他们还是硬着头皮去干。"山棚"下燃了

sisted she had seen everything with her own eyes. The old man didn't know what to believe. He returned home and looked at the "little darlings." They were as sturdy as ever, not a sickly one in the lot.

But the joy that old Tong Bao and his family had been feeling was dampened. They knew Sixth Treasure's words couldn't be entirely without foundation. Their only hope was that Ah Duo and that hussy had played their little games on the porch rather than in the shed!

Old Tong Bao recalled gloomily that the garlic had only put forth three or four shoots. He thought the future looked dark. Hadn't there been times before when the silkworms ate great quantities of leaves and seemed to be growing well, yet dried up and died just when they were ready to spin their cocoons? Yes, often! But Old Tong Bao didn't dare let himself think of such a possibility. To entertain a thought like that, even in the most secret recesses of the mind, would only be inviting bad luck!

IV

The "little darlings" began spinning their cocoons, but Old Tong Bao's family was still in a sweat. Both their money and their energy were completely spent. They still had nothing to show for it; there was no guarantee of their earning any return. Nevertheless, they continued working at top speed. Beneath the racks

火,老通宝和阿四他们伛着腰慢慢地从这边蹲到那边,又从那边蹲到这边。他们听得山棚上有些屑屑索索的细声音,他们就忍不住想笑,过一会儿又不听得了,他们的心就重甸甸地往下沉了。这样地,心是焦灼着,却不敢向山棚上望。偶或他们仰着的脸上淋到了一滴蚕尿了,虽然觉得有点难过,他们心里却快活;他们巴不得多淋一些。

阿多早已偷偷地挑开"山棚"外围着的芦帘望过几次了。小小宝看见,就扭住了阿多,问"宝宝"有没有做茧子。阿多伸出舌头做一个鬼脸,不回答。

"上山"后三天,息火了。四大娘再也忍不住,也偷偷地挑开芦帘角看了一眼,她的心立刻卜地跳了。那是一片雪白,几乎连"缀头"都瞧不见;那是四大娘有生以来从没有见过的"好蚕花"呀!老通宝全家立刻充满了欢笑。现在他们一颗心定下来了!"宝宝"们有良心,四洋一担的叶不是白吃的;他们全家一个月的忍饿失眠总

on which the cocoons were being spun fires had to be kept going to supply warmth. Old Tong Bao and Ah Si, his elder son, their backs bent, slowly squatted first on this side then on that. Hearing the small rustlings of the spinning silkworms, they wanted to smile, and if the sounds stopped for a moment their hearts stopped too. Yet, worried as they were, they didn't dare to disturb the silkworms by looking inside. When the silkworms squirted fluid in their faces as they peered up from beneath the racks, they were happy in spite of the momentary discomfort. The bigger the shower, the better they liked it.

Ah Duo had already peeked several times. Little Bao had caught him at it and demanded to know what was going on. Ah Duo made an ugly face at the child, but did not reply.

After three days of "spinning," the fires were extinguished. Ah Sze's wife could restrain herself no longer. She stole a look, her heart beating fast. Inside, all was white as snow. The brush that had been put in for the silkworms to spin on was completely covered over with cocoons. Ah Si's wife had never seen so successful a " flowering"!

The whole family was wreathed in smiles. They were on solid ground at last! The "little darlings" had proved they had a conscience; they hadn't consumed those mulberry leaves, at four dollars a load, in vain. The family could reap its reward for a month of hunger

算不冤枉,天老爷有眼睛!

同样的欢笑声在村里到处都起来了。今年蚕花娘娘保佑这小小的村子。二三十人家都可以采到七八分,老通宝家更是比众不同,估量来总可以采一个十二三分。

小溪边和稻场上现在又充满了女人和孩子们。这些人都比一个月前瘦了许多,眼眶陷进了,嗓子也发沙,然而都很快活兴奋。她们嘈嘈地谈论那一个月内的"奋斗"时,她们的眼前便时时现出一堆堆雪白的洋钱,她们那快乐的心里便时时闪过了这样的盘算:夹衣和夏衣都在当铺里,这可先得赎出来;过端阳节也许可以吃一条黄鱼。

那晚上荷花和阿多的把戏也是她们谈话的资料。六宝见了人就宣传荷花的"不要脸,送上门去!"男人们听了就粗暴地笑着,女人们念一声佛,骂一句,又说老通宝家总算幸气,没有犯克,那是菩萨保佑,祖宗有灵!

接着是家家都"浪山头"了,各家的至亲好友都来"望山

and sleepless nights. The Old Lord of the Sky had eyes!

Throughout the village, there were many similar scenes of rejoicing. The Silkworm Goddess had been beneficent to the tiny village this year. Most of the two dozen families garnered good crops of cocoons from their silkworms. The harvest of Old Tong Bao's family was well above average.

Again women and children crowded the threshing ground and the banks of the little stream. All were much thinner than the previous month, with eyes sunk in their sockets, throats rasping and hoarse. But everyone was excited, happy. As they chattered about the struggle of the past month, visions of piles of bright silver dollars shimmered before their eyes. Cheerful thoughts filled their minds—they would get their summer clothes out of the pawnshop; at Dragon-Boat Festival perhaps they could eat a fat golden fish....

They talked, too, of the farce enacted by Lotus and Ah Duo a few nights before. Sixth Treasure announced to everyone she met, "That Lotus has no shame at all. She delivered herself right to his door!" Men who heard her laughed coarsely. Women muttered a prayer and called Lotus bad names. They said Old Tong Bao's family could consider itself lucky that a curse hadn't fallen on them. The gods were merciful!

Family after family was able to report a good harvest of cocoons. People visited one another to view the

头"。老通宝的亲家张财发带了小儿子阿九特地从镇上来到村里。他们带来的礼物,是软糕、线粉、梅子、枇把,也有咸鱼。小小宝快活得好像雪天的小狗。

"通宝,你是卖茧子呢,还是自家做丝?"

张老头子拉老通宝到小溪边一棵杨柳树下坐了,这么悄悄地问。这张老头子张财发是出名"会寻快活"的人,他从镇上城隍庙前露天的"说书场"听来了一肚子的疙瘩东西;尤其烂熟的,是《十八路反王,七十二处烟尘》,程咬金卖柴扒,贩私盐出身,瓦岗寨做反王的《隋唐演义》。他向来说话"没正经",老通宝是知道的;所以现在听得问是卖茧子或者自家做丝,老通宝并没把这话看重,只随口回答道:

"自然卖茧子。"

张老头子却拍着大腿叹一口气。忽然他站了起来,用手指着村外那一片秃头桑林后面耸露出来的茧厂的风火墙说道:

"通宝!茧子是采了,那些茧厂的大门还关得紧洞洞呢!今年茧厂不开秤!——十八路反王早已下凡,李世民还没出世;世界不太平!今年茧厂关门,不做生意!"

老通宝忍不住笑了,他不

shining white gossamer. The father of Old Tong Bao's daughter-in-law came from town with his little son. They brought gifts of sweets and fruits and a salted fish. Little Bao was happy as a puppy frolicking in the snow.

The elderly visitor sat with Old Tong Bao beneath a willow beside the stream. He had the reputation in town of a "man who knew how to enjoy life." From hours of listening to the professional story-tetlers in front of the temple, he had learned by heart many of the classic tales of ancient times. He was a great one for idle chatter, and often would say anything that came into his head. Old Tong Bao therefore didn't take him very seriously when he leaned close and queried softly:

"Are you selling your cocoons, or will you spin the silk yourself at home?"

"Selling them, of course," Old Tong Bao replied casually.

The elderly visitor slapped his thigh and sighed, then rose abruptly and pointed at the silk filature rearing up behind the row of mulberries, now quite bald of leaves.

"Tong Bao," he said, "the cocoons are being gathered, but the doors of the silk filatures are shut as tight as ever! They're not buying this year! Ah, all the world is in turmoil! The silk houses are not going to open, I tell you!"

Old Tong Bao couldn't help smiling. He wouldn't

春蚕

肯相信。他怎么能够相信呢?难道那"五步一岗"似的比露天毛坑还要多的茧厂会一齐都关了门不做生意?况且听说和东洋人也已"讲拢",不打仗了,茧厂里驻的兵早已开走。

张老头子也换了话,东拉西扯讲镇里的"新闻",夹着许多"说书场"上听来的什么秦叔宝,程咬金。最后,他代他的东家催那三十块钱的债,为的他是"中人"。

然而老通宝到底有点不放心。他赶快跑出村去,看看"塘路"上最近的两个茧厂,果然大门紧闭,不见半个人;照往年说,此时应该早已摆开了柜台,挂起了一排乌亮亮的大秤。

老通宝心里也着慌了,但是回家去看见了那些雪白发光很厚实硬古古的茧子,他又忍不住嘻开了嘴。上好的茧子!会没有人要,他不相信。并且他还要忙着采茧,还要谢"蚕花利市",他渐渐不把茧厂的事放在心上了。

可是村里的空气一天一天不同了。才得笑了几声的人们现在又都是满脸的愁云。各处

believe it. How could he possibly believe it? There were dozens of silk filatures in this part of the country. Surely they couldn't all shut down? What's more, he had heard that they had made a deal with the Japanese; the Chinese soliders who had been billeted in the silk houses had long since departed.

Changing the subject, the visitor related the latest town gossip, salting it freely with classical aphorisms and quotations from the ancient stories. Finally he got around to the thirty silver dollars borrowed through him as middleman. He said his boss was anxious to be repaid.

Old Tong Bao became uneasy after all. When his visitor had departed, he hurried from the village down the highway to look at the two nearest silk filatures. Their doors were indeed shut; not a soul was in sight. Business was in full swing this time last year, with whole rows of dark gleaming scales in operation.

He felt a little panicky as he returned home. But when he saw those snowy cocoons, thick and hard, pleasure made him smile. What beauties! No one wants them? —Impossible. He still had to hurry and finish gathering the cocoons; he hadn't thanked the gods properly yet. Gradually, he forgot about the silk houses.

But in the village, the atmosphere was changing day by day. People who had just begun to laugh were now all frowns. News was reaching them from town that

春蚕

茧厂都没开门的消息陆续从镇上传来,从"塘路"上传来。往年这时候,"收茧人"像走马灯似的在村里巡回,今年没见半个"收茧人",却换替着来了债主和催粮的差役。请债主们就收了茧子罢,债主们板起面孔不理。

全村子都是嚷骂,诅咒,和失望的叹息!人们做梦也不会想到今年"蚕花"好了,他们的日子却比往年更加困难。这在他们是一个青天的霹雳!并且愈是像老通宝他们家似的,蚕愈养得多,愈好,就愈加困难,——"真正世界变了!"老通宝捶胸跺脚地没有办法。然而茧子是不能搁久了的,总得赶快想法:不是卖出去,就是自家做丝。村里有几家已经把多年不用的丝车拿出来修理,打算自家把茧做成了丝再说。六宝家也打算这么办。老通宝便也和儿子媳妇商量道:

"不卖茧子了,自家做丝!什么卖茧子,本来是洋鬼子行出来的!"

"我们有四百多斤茧子呢,

206

none of the neighbouring silk filatures was opening its doors. It was the same with the houses along the highway. Last year at this time buyers of cocoons were streaming in and out of the village. This year there wasn't a sign of even half a one. In their place came dunning creditors and government tax collectors who promptly froze up if you asked them to take cocoons in payment.

Swearing, curses, disappointed sighs! With such a fine crop of cocoons the villagers had never dreamed that their lot would be even worse than usual! It was as if hailstones dropped out of a clear sky. People like Old Tong Bao, whose crop was especially good, took it hardest of all.

"What is the world coming to!" He beat his breast and stamped his feet in helpless frustration.

But the villagers had to think of something. The cocoons would spoil if kept too long. They either had to sell them or remove the silk themselves. Several families had already brought out and repaired silk reels they hadn't used for years. They would first remove the silk from the cocoons and then see about the next step. Old Tong Bao wanted to do the same.

"We won't sell our cocoons; we'll spin the silk ourselves!" said the old man. "Nobody ever heard of selling cocoons until the foreign devils' companies started the thing!"

Ah Si's wife was the first to object. "We've got over five hundred catties of cocoons here," she retort-

你打算摆几部丝车呀!"

四大娘首先反对了。她这话是不错的。五百斤的茧子可不算少,自家做丝万万干不了。请帮手么?那又得花钱。阿四是和他老婆一条心。阿多抱怨老头子打错了主意,他说:

"早依了我的话,扣住自己的十五担叶,只看一张洋种,多么好!"

老通宝气得说不出话来。

终于一线希望忽又来了。同村的黄道士不知从哪里得的消息,说是无锡脚下的茧厂还是照常收茧。黄道士也是一样的种田人,并非吃十方的"道士",向来和老通宝最说得来。于是老通宝去找那黄道士详细问过了以后,便又和儿子阿四商量把茧子弄到无锡脚下去卖。老通宝虎起了脸,像吵架似的嚷道:

"水路去有三十多九呢!来回得六天!他妈的!简直是充军!可是你有别的办法么?茧子当不得饭吃,蚕前的债又逼紧来!"

阿四也同意了。他们去借了一条赤膊船,买了几张芦席,赶那几天正是好晴,又带了阿多。他们这卖茧子的"远征军"

ed. "Where are you going to get enough reels?"

She was right. Five hundred catties was no small amount. They'd never get finished spinning the silk themselves. Hire outside help? That meant spending money. Ah Si agreed with his wife. Ah Duo blamed his father for planning incorrectly.

"If you listened to me, we'd have raised only one tray of foreign breed and no locals. Then the fifteen loads of leaves from our own mulberry trees would have been enough, and we wouldn't have had to borrow!"

Old Tong Bao was so angry he couldn't speak.

At last a ray of hope appeared. Huang the Priest had heard somewhere that a silk house below the city of Wuxi was doing business as usual. Actually an ordinary peasant, Huang was nicknamed "The Priest" because of the learned airs he affected and his interests in Taoist "magic." Old Tong Bao always got along with him fine. After learning the details from him, Old Tong Bao conferred with his elder son Ah Si about going to Wuxi.

"It's about 270 *li* by water, six days for the round trip," ranted the old man. "Son of a bitch! It's a goddam expedition! But what else can we do? We can't eat the cocoons, and our creditors are pressing hard!"

Ah Si agreed. They borrowed a small boat and bought a few yards of matting to cover the cargo. It was decided that Ah Duo should go along. Taking advantage of the good weather, the cocoon selling "expedi-

就此出发。

五天以后,他们果然回来了;但不是空船,船里还有一筐茧子没有卖出。原来那三十多九水路远的茧厂挑剔得非常苛刻:洋种茧一担只值三十五元,土种茧一担二十元,薄茧不要。老通宝他们的茧子虽然是上好的货色,却也被茧厂里挑剩了那么一筐,不肯收买。老通宝他们实卖得一百十一块钱,除去路上盘川,就剩了整整的一百元,不够偿还买青叶所借的债!老通宝路上气得生病了,两个儿子扶他到家。

打回来的八九十斤茧子,四大娘只好自家做丝了。她到六宝家借了丝车,又忙了五六天。家里米又吃完了。叫阿四拿那丝上镇里去卖,没有人要;上当铺当铺也不收。说了多少好话,总算把清明前当在那里的一石米换了出来。

就是这么着,因为春蚕熟,老通宝一村的人都增加了债!

tionary force" set out.

Five days later, the men returned—but not with an empty hold. They still had one basket of coconns. The silk filature, which they reached after a 270-li journey by water, offered extremely harsh terms— Only thirty-five dollars a load for foreign breed, twenty for local; thin cocoons not wanted at any price. Although their cocoons were all first class, the people at the silk house picked and chose, leaving them one basket of rejects. Old Tong Bao and his sons received a hundred and ten dollars for the sale, ten of which had to be spent as travel expenses. The hundred dollars remaining was not even enough to pay back what they had borrowed for that last thirty loads of mulberry leaves! On the return trip, Old Tong Bao became ill with rage. His sons carried him into the house.

Ah Si's wife had no choice but to take the ninety odd catties they had brought back and reel the silk from the cocoons herself. She borrowed a few reels from Sixth Treasure's family and worked for six days. All their rice was gone now. Ah Si took the silk into town, but no one would buy it. Even the pawnshop didn't want it. Only after much pleading was he able to persuade the pawnbroker to take it in exchange for a load of rice they had pawned before Clear and Bright.

That's the way it happened. Because they raised a crop of spring silkworms, the people in Old Tong Bao's village got deeper into debt. Old Tong Bao's family

老通宝家为的养了五张布子的蚕,又采了十多分的好茧子,就此白赔上十五担叶的桑地和三十块钱的债!一个月光景的忍饿熬夜还都不算!

1932 年 11 月 1 日

raised five trays and gathered a splendid harvest of cocoons. Yet they ended up owing another thirty silver dollars and losing their mortgaged mulberry trees—to say nothing of suffering a month of hunger and sleepless nights in vain!

November 1, 1932